Kansas City Breakdown

Kansas City Breakdown

by

Russell Thayer
&
M.E. Proctor

Book 2 of the Tom Keegan & Vivian Davis Series

Cowboy Jamboree Press
good grit lit.

No AI was used in the creation of this work.
First Edition
ISBN: 979-8-90243-183-1

Cover Design: Frank Vatel
Interior Design: Adam Van Winkle

Cowboy Jamboree Press
good grit lit.

www.cowboyjamboreemagazine.com/books

From Reader Reviews for Book 1 of the series:
Bop City Swing

"Russell Thayer and M.E. Proctor's *Bop City Swing* masterfully harkens back to the noir classics of yester-year, with the soulfulness of a Charlie Parker riff on a foggy night. *Bop City Swing* is a riveting cat and mouse tale pitting two contemporary grit noir characters—Proctor's formidable Detective Tom Keegan and Thayer's deadly femme fatale, 'Gunselle'—in a tale that twists and turns like a brakeless ride down Mulholland Drive in a 1940s Caddy. Thayer and Proctor have given us a classic contemporary take on old school noir that leaves the reader so satisfied they'll want to fire up a Chesterfield and pour a double bourbon in the afterglow!"

"Noir fiction has a distinct cadence and ambience all its own. It deploys a variety of plot standards to achieve its dark effects. *Bop City Swing* showcases a cast of memorable suspects searching for answers—if not salvation—in the lurid depths of the eternal demi-monde. Its authors, Russell Thayer and M.E. Proctor, masterfully weave their story with such savvy, skill, and love of the genre that their resulting *Bop City Swing* is a Grit Lit classic!"

"*Bop City Swing* is a pitch-perfect, period-piece mystery that seamlessly fuses the writing styles of two of our neo-noir greats: M.E. Proctor, whose short-stories I've described elsewhere as the lovechild of Ruth Rundell and Ray Bradbury, and Russell Thayer, whose repeating antihero 'Gunselle' simultaneously creates and exemplifies the niche of the professional hitwoman of the black-and-white era."

"*Bop City Swing* plunges readers into the jazz-rich atmosphere of post-WWII San Francisco, bringing the 1950s vividly to life. The story follows two parallel investigators—a homicide detective, Tom Keegan, racing to solve a political assassination at a fundraiser, and 'Gunselle', a female contract killer frustrated that someone else beat her to the assignment. On the surface it might seem like an uneasy alliance, but it works and creates a tight, tension-filled narrative that moves forward. The plot moves briskly, with enough twists to keep tension high without sacrificing any historical detail of 1951 San Francisco (the city itself is an important character in the book)."

"I can't get enough of crime novels set in the 50s, so this collaboration between Thayer and Proctor was a must read. Thayer brings his character 'Gunselle' and Proctor brings her character Tom Keegan, and the mix is an explosive one. Pulp charm, plenty of atmosphere, and music in the violence. Wonderful read."

"My goodness, the title hints at the time period you're stepping into but not at all at the fast paced hard-boiled story wrapped around it. *Bop City Swing* hits the ground running with shadowy bars, flowing booze and a bloody death within the first few pages. Proctor and Thayer blend their styles to the clipped and stripped prose of the best hard-boiled fiction from Hammett and Chandler. It works so well that I found myself pounding through the pages to get to the end. Such a great read. I cannot recommend it enough."

"I was doing a cheap sneaky job for people I didn't like, but that's what you hire out for, chum. They pay the bills, you dig the dirt."

—Raymond Chandler, Playback

1. Mid-April

Two men in threadbare dungarees sat down on the other side of the table. They lit cigarettes and waited. Their creased leather jackets hung open over tight white undershirts. Gunselle noted the thick pectoral muscles on display. These guys worked hard for a living. One of them wore wire-rimmed spectacles. Both had fresh haircuts. They were clean-shaven and jumpy.

Gunselle used to meet potential clients at a small neighborhood Italian restaurant. Now she rotated her office through a couple of bars, when she met anyone at all. Tonight, it was a booth in the rear of the Hunt-In Club at 16th and Guerrero. She had wine. The men drank beer.

"Let's get down to business," she said. Her blond wig was starting to itch and it made her impatient.

"What are your politics?" asked the man with the glasses. The other guy watched the door.

"I don't have any politics. Can't afford it."

"That's a bullshit answer," said the guy watching the door.

"Take it or leave it, buddy boy. I've done jobs conservatively." Her eyes moved from man to man. "And liberally."

"This is an important one."

"Then I hope it pays well. Give me a hint."

"Truman."

"No. How much does it pay?"

"Twenty thousand, if you're successful."

"I'd need half up front." She took a sip of wine. With money like that she could retire and open the dress shop she'd been thinking about. Far from San Francisco. Someplace warm where it didn't rain so much.

"We can give you five up front. The rest comes once that son-of-a-bitch is dead."

"It's ten, but why bother? Our tired leader declared

that he isn't running again. He's a lame duck. Read a newspaper. They sell them on every street corner."

"We want him gone before his term is over."

Gunselle raised an eyebrow. "Who is we?"

"You wouldn't understand," said the guy who wasn't wearing glasses.

"Because I'm just a dumb broad?"

"Because you thought about the money before you thought about the job."

She had her priorities, and his comeback told her what she wanted to know. "You're Commies."

"We're Americans who love our country, and there are a lot of us who are sickened by what it's become."

She chuckled. Dreamy-eyed idealists. "Win elections, what's stopping you? Change some minds. That's how it's done in America." She had seen every kind of client over the years. They hired her for reasons that mattered little to her. Her standard of measurement was the price they were willing to pay for the job. Twenty grand? These boobs understood how Capitalism worked.

"Yeah, do it on the square. For the long haul. That's pretty funny coming from someone like you."

"What's that supposed to mean?" She took another sip of wine and resisted the urge to scratch her scalp under the wig.

"I bet in the past some sad-faced gal hired you to plug her husband, the devoted father of her kids, for a hundred bucks. Is that the American way?"

"If that's what I charged her. It's cheaper and more effective than divorce." She winked. "But we're not here to talk about me. What do you have in mind for twenty grand?"

"Truman is scheduled to speak at a meeting of the San Francisco Stock and Bond Exchange on June 12. You could take him then."

"I'm sure Bess will be thrilled. Where is that meeting taking place?"

"At their lunch club on the tenth floor of the Pacific

Stock Exchange building. It's exclusive, you'll have to disguise yourself as a waitress or something."

"Don't tell me how to do my job." Gunselle pondered the location. "That's the club with the Diego Rivera mural. I'm sorry I won't get to see it."

"What?"

She leaned toward them, over the table. "Look, I don't care if you slimy Reds are pissed off about the war in Korea, the Truman Doctrine, the NATO thing, the Marshall Plan, or the niggling loyalty tests the feds are making every damn employee take right now. I'm concerned with the kind of heat that starching the President would bring down on me. In the town where I live." She pulled off the wig and dropped it on the floor next to her chair. "God, I hate this thing." She was Vivian again. She ruffled her hair and brushed it over her ears. "It's a good offer, but I have to disappoint you, comrades. It's too close to home." She finished her wine. "Here's some free advice. When you're ready to build your labor camps, I recommend Idaho. It's the perfect place to be miserable."

"You shouldn't believe government propaganda."

The young man with the spectacles handed her a card with a number scribbled on the blank side. She turned it over. It was one of the cards she'd had printed in the late forties. *Gunselle for Hire.*

"Think about our proposal and call us if you change your mind. We give you a week."

She pocketed the card and picked up her wig. She stuffed most of it into her purse and got to her feet.

"Don't hold your breath."

2. Saturday, April 26

Gales of laughter greeted Tom Keegan's arrival at the office. He stopped in the door, not fully awake before his second cup of coffee. He checked his clothes for a possible wardrobe mishap. Everything seemed fine. His fly was zipped, and his trench coat wasn't inside out. He wasn't sure the socks matched but that was a minor offense.

"What's going on? What did I do?"

That caused another volley of cackles. The squad room was more crowded than usual. Most desks were manned, a rare occurrence so early in the morning. Despite the hour, a layer of cigarette smoke floated near the ceiling. The detectives must have been at it all night. For once Tom hadn't joined them. After three late shifts in a row, he'd earned a night off.

"I won!" Al 'Matt' Matteotti, Tom's partner, whooped in glee. "Hand over the sawbucks, losers."

Tom's brain was clear enough he could read between the lines. He dropped his hat on the desk and hung up his coat. "Considering I helped you make a bundle you could share the haul with me."

"That would be collusion." Matt counted the ten-dollar bills. Six. Nothing to sniff at.

"What was the bet?"

Matt pointed at Tom's shirt. He winked. "Blue tie."

Tom stared. "You guys must be really bored." Under his breath, he muttered. "You're a vile crook, Matteotti."

Matt shot him a wide-eyed innocent look. "I had a feeling you'd spend the night at Rachel's place. Last time you had a blue tie going in and a green one coming out. There was a good chance the blue tie would be back in rotation, laundered and ironed. You should vary your routine, partner."

Tom pulled files out of his desk drawer and resumed the task where he'd left it the evening before. Sometimes reading the notes again with fresh eyes shook something loose. "I salute your powers of observation. Might want to apply them to the job for a change."

Matt pocketed the money and held out a hand for the documents. "Give me half."

They worked in companionable silence occasionally interrupted by the ring of a telephone. There were enough cops around that neither Tom nor Matt bothered picking up. That blessed indifference to phone summons couldn't last.

A detective shouted from the other side of the room. "Hey, Keegan, chief wants to see you."

It always meant more work.

"He didn't ask for me," Matt said. "This one's all yours, buddy."

"You're a swell partner. Sharing when it suits you. Making money off my back."

It was easygoing. Matt was a solid partner and sorely missed when a nasty fall with major bone breakage put him out of contention for several months. Tom had been flying solo when he got embroiled in the Charles Forrester case the year before. He sometimes wondered how it would have turned out if Matt had been by his side.

Tom took the steps three at a time. When the chief called, his detectives ran. He didn't bother to knock and walked right in. He took stock of the scene.

The chief sat behind the massive barrier of his oak desk, puffing on a cigar, Pete Delgado, the vice squad supervisor, was perched on the corner of the desk, and two strangers in identical dark suits occupied the visitors' chairs. FBI. They had the clean-cut look that was de rigueur in Hoover's organization. Pete Delgado, with his wrinkled clothes, fatigue-rimmed eyes, and unshaven chin was scruffy. Tom knew he cut a sharp figure in his gray suit and crisp blue tie. He slept well last night. Delgado should be off duty and heading for his bed. The expression on his lined face spoke volumes. *Get me the hell out of here.*

The chief pointed at the two visitors. "Special Agents Burdon and Stansted. They have a job for you, Tommy."

He was immediately on guard. The Bureau had the reputation of hogging the plum assignments while saddling local law enforcement with menial chores. Not to mention that they took all the credit afterwards with fat headlines in the papers. Tom had no intention of being anybody's errand boy or patsy. He was fine working homicide cases.

"What kind of job? My plate is full, Chief."

"I know, but this is important. Lay it out, Burdon."

He was the senior special agent, older than his colleague, with graying hair, a deep line of worry slashed between the eyebrows, and the kind of aggressive chin that would go through doors before the rest of his body did.

With a hint of a sigh, Tom crossed the room and leaned on the windowsill. Catching a sliver of view through the blinds gave him an illusion of freedom. Whatever headache the feds had in store for him, it helped to remember there was life out there. He wondered where Rachel was headed this morning. The *Chronicle* offices weren't visible from where he stood. She never told him what stories she was working on, just like he didn't leak investigation details. Unless that served a purpose. He smiled at the thought. And winced. Burdon's shrill voice cut through his daydreaming.

"An informant in Texas came to us. The Mob is meeting in Kansas City next week. Something major. We want to infiltrate the proceedings."

Tom lit a cigarette. He blew smoke toward the ceiling to add to the perennial gray cushion up there. The feds didn't smoke, that filthy habit was discouraged. The cloud was the chief's doing.

"A crooks' convention in Missouri and a source in Texas. What are you doing in San Francisco?"

"One of the attendees is a local guy, Michael Abati. He'll travel to Kansas City from San Francisco by train. The man's afraid of flying. It's a unique opportunity to get close to him."

Abati was Mafia boss Tony Lima's second in command, involved in all kinds of trafficking, and slippery. Nailing him was one of the chief's obsessions. It explained why he was listening to the FBI. It also explained Pete Delgado's presence. The vice squad locked horns with Lima and his goons on a daily basis. Delgado knew the local mob's business inside out.

"Hoover has changed his tune on the Syndicate?" Tom said. "I thought the Mob was a figment of our imagination."

Burdon shrugged. His colleague, Stansted, shifted in his seat, annoyed. Feds were prickly about Hoover's quirks. Organized crime was only one of their boss's hang-ups. His men had plenty of reasons to be sensitive to gibes.

"We're following up on reliable intelligence," Burdon snapped.

"If you already have an insider, what do you need Abati for?"

"We want to put somebody in who can feed us information in real time," Burdon said.

"They plan to put a girl on the train and have her cozy up to Abati.," Pete Delgado said, disgusted. "Get him so enamored that he'll take her to the meeting and spill the beans on the pillow. It's suicide. The man is a stone-cold killer."

"A girl? One of ours?"

Delgado nodded. He was worse than tired. Wrung out.

"With appropriate support, of course." Burdon pointed a finger at Tom. "Yours. You come highly recommended."

"You're out of your mind."

"Told them. They're not listening," Delgado said. "The man's a murderer. He should be behind bars, waiting for the gas. I'm not putting one of our auxiliaries within spitting distance of that animal."

Burdon dismissed the comment with a hand wave. "It's a simple play. Show a little leg and cleavage, pour a few drinks, and get the guy to brag. They all brag when they're properly motivated. Don't you have a pretty one smart enough to do that kind of job?"

"It's nonsense," Tom said. "Sending a woman to seduce Abati, with his armed bodyguards in the corridor, when his mind is on a meeting with people who won't hesitate to put a slug in his head if he doesn't measure up. He isn't a slow-witted gunsel, Burdon. He won't fall for a curvy broad who appears out of nowhere. He'll be damn suspicious. And she'll end up dead, by the side of the tracks."

Burdon smirked. "You're saying you can't protect her?"

The man was trying to get a rise out of Tom and he wasn't subtle about it. "If I have to protect her, the game is over. Supposing the game even got off the ground to begin with."

"Won't," Delgado mumbled. "My auxiliaries can lure a john from a street corner or slip a mickey in a dark bar. They can't do this."

Burdon had a temper and it was running thin. "You've made your point, Delgado, more than once. I have my orders. The operation will proceed, with or without your cooperation."

Tom dropped the stub of his cigarette in an empty coffee cup on the chief's desk. "Count me out. I have work to do." He took two steps toward the door.

"Keegan!" The chief's bark wasn't loud. It didn't have to be. "Special Agent Burdon hasn't told you everything."

"What a surprise."

Tom pulled out his cigarette pack and lit a fresh one. He handed the sticks to Delgado who hadn't moved from his perch on the desk corner, a prime spot that put him higher than the two federal agents.

"I don't know how the Bureau runs its business, Burdon," the chief said, "but here, we don't keep secrets. When I send my men out on a job, I want them to have all the information they need to make decisions."

It was a load of hooey but neither Tom nor Delgado blinked.

The FBI agent wriggled in his chair. "We've been made aware of threats on the President's life. He's been advised to limit his public appearances, but he insists on opening the Kansas City Livestock Show and Rodeo next week. He'll be in town for a few days, while the Mob meeting is taking place."

Tom took a puff of his cigarette. "Now I understand why Hoover is suddenly interested in the Syndicate."

"Security will be tight. Airports, train stations. We'll have eyes on the Mob bosses at all times. We don't yet know where they're gathering, but it's only a matter of time."

"Don't tell me Hoover wants to infiltrate the Mob meeting because he thinks they plan to bump off Truman." Tom chuckled. "If these guys had a contract on the Prez, they would be a thousand miles away from Kansas City."

Burdon's face was even more pinched than before. "I'm not privy to the Director's thoughts. My hierarchy sees this as an opportunity. We'll have all this manpower on site, with close surveillance in place. It would be a shame not to get intelligence out of it. We'll be in breathing distance of some of the most notorious gangsters in the country, with a chance to find out what they're up to. Abati offers us a soft way in."

"Soft." Delgado shook his head in disbelief.

"There's an easier way to get what you want," Tom said. "Grab one of these goons and work him over. He'll recite the Rosary."

Burdon huffed. "We don't do that."

"No. You'd rather risk a girl's life."

The chief knocked on his desk. "Gentlemen, let's see if we can figure this out. And haul your ass off my desk, Delgado, I'm tired of looking at it." He leaned back in his chair and the tortured piece of furniture groaned. "Burdon and Stansted have instructions. Somebody dreamed up a plan. It's boneheaded but we're stuck with it. The Bureau wants San Francisco PD to supply the undercover asset and her handler. We've had dealings with Mike Abati, we know his crew, so that makes some sense. But we don't have a suitable girl on the payroll." He raised a hand to block the objection he could see coming from the FBI senior agent. "Delgado knows his people, Burdon. I trust him."

"With all due respect, Chief, it doesn't explain what I'm doing here," Tom said.

"You can think on the run and I have a feeling it will be needed. You're going to KC and it's not up for debate. Now, who's the girl gonna be? Delgado's auxiliaries are out. Ideas?"

Stansted cleared his throat. "What if we used a professional?"

Delgado burst out laughing. "A hooker? Good luck finding one who's not working for Lima already ... and an honest one, who won't sell us to Abati first chance she gets."

Tom was pacing the room to work out his irritation. A trip to Missouri to take care of a woman in a nest of mobsters. Talk about a rotten assignment. "We can recruit out of town, Pete. Or make a deal with a chick who needs forgiveness. Clean record, bus ticket to somewhere. Chance at a new life. That sort of thing."

Delgado pondered. "Dolls stuck in desperate situations aren't too bright, generally, unless they're unlucky. You don't want to be saddled with one of those. It'll help if she's endowed. A decent rack, a perky ass, some personality, and balls. Lotsa balls. She can't be intimidated by the heavies." He sighed. "A rare bird."

Tom's wanderings had led him back to the office window. He hoped Rachel enjoyed her morning more than he did. "Does Abati have a regular squeeze?"

"He's a family man." Delgado smirked.

"He doesn't stray?" Burdon sounded worried.

Pete Delgado grinned. "A steady mistress costs money and Abati is a tightwad. When he's in the mood, he helps himself to one of Lima's stable girls, meals ready-to-eat, free snacks."

"Is he taking one with him on the trip?" Tom asked.

"Not that we know," Burdon said.

"We better find out." It's what Tom feared. The feds didn't know much. Slapdash homework. "Who will be traveling with him, Pete?"

"Muscle for sure. He won't show up in KC without an entourage. It's a status thing. Abati is mid-level. Two gorillas to handle the luggage would be my guess. One of them will certainly be Leo, the Nutcracker. He's a vicious piece of work. Loyal and smart, unfortunately."

"He's a sidekick," Burdon said. "Whatever his boss decides, he'll fall in line."

The more Tom thought about the job, the more he was convinced they needed an exceptional player to pull it off. Sass and brass aplenty. A rare bird indeed who could keep a cool head with her life on the line. He knew somebody, all right, but would she agree to do it?

"How much hard cash can you put on the table, Burdon? You need special talent. Expertise is expensive. How much are you prepared to cough up to find out what the Mob is cooking?"

3. Sunday, April 27

"You're up earlier than usual," Vivian said.

The clock on the wall showed it was almost lunch time. Maggie, in a white cotton robe, her copper hair matted, slumped at the chrome-edged kitchen table with a mug of coffee cupped in her palms. Vivian's empty breakfast bowl had been sitting there for three hours already.

"What are you so dolled up for?" Maggie said.

"I have a lunch date."

Vivian wore a smart blue suit over a tight black sweater. Her dark hair was brushed to a bright sheen, and she had taken a bath while Maggie slept in. The girl had been out until two, at a jam session in the Fillmore. She was an in-demand piano player, a budding jazz celebrity.

"What is this thing called lunch?" Maggie yawned, exposing crooked teeth.

"It happens every day around noon. Do you have a hangover?"

"No."

"Because if I find out you've been drinking, you'll be out on your scrawny ass. Right down onto the pavement. You might fly out that living room window if you're not careful."

"I know. I'm not going to mess it up."

Vivian had taken Maggie in a few months before, when the girl was released from the hospital after multiple surgeries. She'd been stabbed in the stomach and had been a heavy drinker long before that. The knife wound had closed, her organs were repaired, but the drinking was a wound that could reopen at any time. Vivian wished the girl would stay away from nightclubs and find a square job, but she was a superb talent. Everyone said so. The temptation to fall into drink again must be strong in the clubs where she played and everyone was flying high. Maggie stayed home Sunday through Thursday, practicing all day on the upright piano recently delivered to the apartment. Friday and Saturday nights worried Vivian. Dark things tended to bloom in the midnight hours.

"Good. I want you here."

"For how long?" Maggie's pale blue eyes peered over the rim of her mug.

There was wistfulness in the girl's tone. A touch of anxiety. Maggie's life was a series of traumatic events. She'd survived an internment camp in the Philippines, an errant existence in San Francisco, shady clubs and shadier people, alcohol and drugs. Living with Vivian was more comfort and stability than she had known in years. She must fear it wouldn't last. And Vivian had laid down stern rules.

"For as long as you want." Vivian wished the girl would tell her what bugged her. Was she lonely? "You have a home here, but I'm not family. Aren't you ever curious about what happened to your mother?" Maggie had mentioned a baby brother once, and that her father had been murdered by a Japanese soldier.

"No."

"I'll bet she cries herself to sleep wondering what happened to her talented daughter."

"She doesn't care a whit about me." Maggie snorted. "As if you never made anybody cry."

Vivian took her breakfast bowl to the sink. She rinsed the dish and dried her hands on a towel. Silence felt heavy in the kitchen.

"I'm sorry," Maggie said. "Who's your lunch date?"

"Remember that cop?" Vivian was happy to change the subject.

"The one who makes you wet your pants? Keegan? Why? What's he got on you?"

"I guess I'll find out."

The message from her answering service was short and sweet. *Meet me tomorrow. Balboa Café. Noon. Keegan.*

"You think you're going to get him into bed after your usual three glasses of wine at lunch?"

"I doubt seduction is on the menu. And never mind how many glasses of wine I drink at lunch."

"Are you going to kill him?"

"I'm fond of him. Someone would have to pay me an awful lot of money ..."

"A thousand dollars?"

"Don't be stupid."

"Two thousand?"

"Certainly not."

"Three thousand?"

"NO!"

"Five thousand?"

"Oh, shut up."

Vivian's eyes fell on a small painting hanging crooked on the wall. It was the portrait of a young woman with dark hair piled on her head. She was bent over an ironing board, perspiring, exhausted. Vivian straightened the frame with her trigger finger.

"Is that a real Degas?" Maggie asked.

"It is."

Because of that painting, Vivian would never have to kill Detective Tom Keegan. Not for five thousand dollars, not for anything. She lifted her shoe onto a chair and adjusted her stocking. She smoothed her skirt and picked up her purse.

"Did you steal that painting?"

"I earned it."

"How?"

"You know how."

Vivian remembered that contract. She remembered all of them. She was at the top of her game then, an in-demand assassin with an impeccable professional record. Those days were gone, the jobs thin on the ground. She blamed it on the drug trafficking rampant in the city. Snow merchants hired junkies to take out their competition. At half her price, no planning, no subtlety. Expertise wasn't appreciated anymore. It wasn't worth a damn.

*

The Balboa Café was on Fillmore, not far from the apartment. Vivian took a corner booth and ordered a glass of red wine.

She chewed on breadsticks while waiting for the detective. What could Keegan possibly want? She hadn't seen him since the Forrester investigation. She didn't think the lunch invitation was a trap to nab her. After all, she'd saved his life.

Tom walked in, a half hour late. Vivian was on her second glass of wine. She caught his eye and waved him over to the table. He hung his fedora on a hook attached to the post of the booth, and settled in. He looked good.

"Hi, handsome."

"Don't start. I'm here on business."

"Are you eating? How's your lovely girlfriend? Are you still happy with her?"

"Yes. Fine. And yes."

The waitress stopped by. They ordered soup and sandwiches. Vivian asked for another glass of wine.

"Have a beer, Detective."

"I'm on duty."

"You're at lunch." Vivian told the waitress: "He'll have a glass of wine." If he didn't drink it, she would.

The waitress departed.

"So," said Vivian, "we meet again. It's good to see you." She meant it. Looking at him tickled the nerves below her waist. "I suppose I should inquire as to *why* I'm seeing you again. You said you wouldn't bother me if I didn't bother you."

"I have something that might interest you."

"Rachel's not cutting it in that department?"

He sighed. "It's a job."

"I don't work for the police."

"For the feds. Washington DC."

"I don't work for the feds either. Tell Hoover's honeys to shove their offer."

"They haven't made an offer yet. At this point it's just an idea I'm playing with in my head."

She rested her chin on her steepled hands and smiled. "I like that head of yours. Thinking it was almost bashed in ... What's the idea?"

The waitress brought Tom's wine. He pushed the glass toward Vivian.

"The FBI wants information on a Mob conference. They want to know what the goons are up to. They suggested enlisting one of our regular girls, the auxiliaries we use to bust johns or get guys chatty in bars, but these dames aren't up to it. I told the feds I might know someone in town with acting experience. Retired from the movies."

She bit on a breadstick. It made a sharp snapping sound. "I'm not old enough to be retired from anything."

"The job requires brains and poise. Icy nerves. Which you have in spades." He shot her a thin smile. "On top of the rest of the package."

A rare compliment. After calling her 'retired'. "What does it pay?"

The waitress brought a tray and set down the food. Vivian took in the smell of the tomato soup. The turkey and Swiss would go well with it. She was hungry. Sitting at a table with Tom, almost a date, awoke all sorts of cravings.

"They'll put a grand on it."

Vivian's laughter was so loud that diners across the room turned to look at her.

"A grand? Are you kidding? I wouldn't take out a child molester for that piddling amount. A grand!" She laughed again.

"The job involves traveling to Kansas City by train." He looked Vivian in the eye as he bit into his tuna sandwich. "With me."

She leaned on the back of the booth, pensive. Did his voice drop an octave or was she imagining it? All their conversations had taken place at night. It was interesting to be around him in daylight for a change. She wished she could put warmth in these cool gray eyes.

"You know how to sweeten a deal, Tommy. The music of wheels on rails, the soft shift of cars in the curves." She had a sip of wine. "When I imagine us together, a narrow bunk in a sleeper car doesn't spring to mind. Too damn uncomfortable.

What's the catch?" The soup was delicious. She should come back to the café and bring Maggie.

He put his sandwich back on the plate and searched his pockets for his cigarettes, popped one out of the pack, and lit up. He waved at the waitress. "Can I have a cup of coffee, please? Black."

The girl was back a minute later. Vivian had to smile at the dreamy look she gave Tom. He was oblivious, preoccupied with mobsters and feds. She wondered how he handled the interrogation of female suspects. How would he interview her if she was in the hot seat, with a blinding light in her face, like they did in the movies? She shook the thought away and munched on her sandwich.

"Do you know Mike Abati?" He took a long drag of his cigarette and blew the smoke away from her.

"Lima's enforcer?"

Tom nodded. "You ever met him?"

"I've seen him with his gorillas in clubs and hotel lobbies. We never spoke."

"Would he recognize you?"

"How good would I be at what I do if goons, and others, knew what I really look like? I meet with lowly intermediaries; I never deal with the bosses. They keep my kinds of services at arms' length. Abati is in the feds' crosshairs?"

"He's taking the train to Kansas City for the Mob conclave. The FBI believes Abati can be enticed to reveal what's going on in there. As you said, the music of the wheels on the tracks, a sleeper car ..." He crushed his cigarette in the ashtray. "The feds think gangsters are stupid meatheads that grunt instead of talk."

Vivian chuckled. "They're not totally wrong."

"Abati is a killer, traveling with brutes, to go meet with a gaggle of murderers. He also has a functioning brain and an acute sense of self-preservation. It'll take more than a bimbo to fool him."

"So, you thought I had the right credentials. I can get

flat on my back, open my legs, and remain composed and focused on the mission. Tits with a side of brains." She shook her head. "You have some nerve."

He took a deep breath and exhaled slowly. "I don't like it one bit but I've been drafted. The feds are committed to the plan. I don't want to lead a girl to the slaughter, Vivian. You're tough and you're clever. Together, we can make a dumb scheme work and walk out of it alive."

"It's not like the FBI to go half-cocked. What are they really after?"

Tom shrugged. "Hoover is having the vapors because Truman will be in Kansas City for the Rodeo, and the Mob is meeting next door. He might have visions of a Saint Valentine's Day Massacre with the Prez dodging bullets. I don't know, Viv. I tried to get out of it, but I don't have a choice. Orders. Click your heels. Suck it up. If you tell me to go to hell, I'll understand."

They kept silent for a while. Vivian finished her lunch. She was thinking hard. A high-profile hit in San Francisco was out of the question, but Missouri … Truman schmoozing with his local buddies, visitors flocking to Kansas City for the festivities, a gaggle of mobsters to add to the chaos … It wouldn't be easy, but easy jobs didn't pay.

Tom pushed away what was left of his food. He offered her the pack of cigarettes.

"I don't smoke, remember?" She picked up his unwanted sandwich half and wolfed it down. "I'll do it for five grand. Do a little math. It's a bargain when you look at the hours I'll put in." She smiled. "Because it's you and you asked nicely."

"The feds pinch pennies. They're offering one thousand."

"What? No slush fund? Go shake a bookie, raid a gambling den. There's so much sin for sale in this town, can't you find a few grand under the carpets?"

Tom folded his napkin. "I shouldn't have called."

Vivian didn't want him to go yet. She enjoyed sitting in

that booth, looking at him, listening to his voice. And the Truman job … maybe.

"We can still make a deal. You could do me a favor."

His reaction was sharp, immediate. "I can't grant you absolution. You have to go higher up for that." His mouth was a tight hard line.

He might as well have slapped her. "Damn you, Keegan. The upright copper? You never slipped, played loose with the law, punched too hard? There's no gray in your life?"

He leaned in with his face close to hers. "I'm having lunch with a killer-for-hire. It doesn't come much grayer, Miss Davis."

She pushed back from the table. She strained to keep her voice down. "I believe we can find an arrangement that won't tarnish your precious badge."

"That would surprise me," he muttered.

Vivian urged herself to remain calm. She pushed Truman and the Commies to the back of her mind. If she wanted to stay in that Kansas City game, she had to come up with something that would convince Tom she had a change of heart. An idea was forming. She thought of the conversation with Maggie, at the apartment, and the girl's prickly response when she mentioned her mother.

"You could do something for Maggie."

He frowned. "The girl's in trouble?"

Pure Tom Keegan. He wouldn't lift a finger to get her out of jail but he'd jump in the Bay to save a drowning kitten. "She's been down in the blue layer for months. It worries me."

"Her injuries were serious. Recovery takes time. Not just the body, the mind too."

"I doubt that's it. It's more how her life has changed. Living with me, the success with the music. The trying to stay off the booze and drugs. I think she's scared she's going to fail, and she's keeping it all inside. She never talks about the people she's lost."

"Do you ever talk about your past?"

Vivian shrugged the comment aside. "It's different. You have contacts in the administration, law enforcement, veterans' groups and such. You could make calls and find what's left of her family. I believe her mother is still in Manila. It might do some good. I don't know."

"Margaret Bates. She's British, right? You could go to the Consulate. Take her along."

"I don't want her to know I'm doing this."

Tom looked dubious. "There is no guarantee inquiries will deliver anything. Millions of people were displaced."

"Just have a look. If there are no results, that's an answer of sorts."

"It'll take weeks, Viv, months. Glaciers move faster than government officials."

Vivian smiled. "And the Mob meeting is imminent, is that it?"

"In a few days."

"I trust you'll do the right thing and give Maggie your best. Do we have a deal?"

"It's hardly fair," Tom said. "You may be risking your life, and all you get in exchange is a promise."

"I expect you to protect me, baby. And you don't know what kind of mess you'll find when you start poking into Maggie's life."

Tom smiled. "You're one wily customer."

"That's why you're hiring me. How do we work this?"

He lit a fresh cigarette. "I'm your contact. When you have information, you pass it to me. I'll be close."

"No way I can pack anything more lethal than nail scissors."

"I'll carry the artillery."

"It's like telling Jonah to go explore the inside of a whale, while tying a rope around his waist with promises to pull him back if needed." Other biblical equivalents came to mind. Daniel in the lions' den was most fitting.

"I will not let harm come to you, Vivian."

Define harm. Abati wasn't likely to sit at her feet

reading poetry. "You won't seal the deal with a kiss, will you? Does Rachel know about this Missouri excursion?"

"I don't discuss my caseload with Rachel."

"Of course you don't." She plucked the cigarette from his mouth, took a quick hit, and crushed the stub in her soup bowl. "Very well. But I will not board that train unannounced and rely on luck to put me on Mike Abati's path. I will be *invited,* Tommy, expected with erotic anticipation. It's the least I can do to bring the man to his knees."

"Invited? How?"

"Meet me at Pepper's tomorrow night, around ten."

4. Monday, April 28

Vivian stared at the empty wastebasket in her bedroom. What had she done with that card? She pushed everything around on the top of her dresser, went through the pockets of every jacket in her closet, opened and slammed the door of the medicine cabinet, kicked over the metal can in the bathroom, and banged around in the kitchen.

"What is wrong?" Maggie shouted from behind her closed bedroom door.

"Nothing. Go back to sleep. It's eleven o'clock in the morning. Jesus Christ. I shouldn't have to tiptoe around."

"You're not tiptoeing around. You sound like a delivery truck rolling over at forty miles an hour."

"Did you empty the wastebaskets?"

"Yes."

"Why?"

"Because you said you'd put a bullet in my head if I didn't get off my lazy ass and do it. I believe those were your exact words."

"When did you manage to get all this work done?"

"Yesterday, when the super buzzed for trash. I dumped everything in a grocery bag with the kitchen scraps and set it in the box. A bag from Lucky, to be precise. What did you lose?"

Vivian opened the door to the dumbwaiter. The bag had already gone down to the incinerator. She raced to the basement. The door of the incinerator room was unlocked. The super usually emptied the dumbwaiter boxes the morning after alerting the tenants. She had beaten him to the room. The air was hot and ripe. Bags of trash stood next to the incinerator. Vivian knocked the bags over until she found one with 'Lucky' printed on the side. She emptied it onto the concrete floor. The number on the card stared back at her through a smear of blood-red catsup.

Maggie was still in bed when Vivian came back to the apartment. She picked up the phone and dialed the local number. The phone rang three times before a woman answered.

"Keller residence."

Vivian could hear a baby wailing in the background. "Hello. Is Mr. Keller at home?"

"Who may I say is calling?"

Vivian couldn't tell the woman that she'd met her husband a week ago at a bar on Potrero Hill and she couldn't use her real name. Or Gunselle.

"Tell him it's Mrs. Truman. Not Bess, that old hag. It's work-related."

"At the dockyard? I didn't know women worked down there."

"I'm with the union."

"Oh. I'll fetch him."

Vivian sighed. Keller. Dockyard. Union. He wouldn't be hard to locate after the hit, if things went south and she needed to clean up the mess. The other guy would probably be just as easy to find. These Reds were clowns.

"Hello, Alice," said the familiar male voice. "It's good to hear from you." The wife must still be within earshot.

"Hey, buddy boy. Something has come up. Truman will be in Kansas City, early May. I'll be there on business. I could add him to the agenda, if you're still interested. It'll be earlier than you wanted."

"The earlier the better."

"We have to review logistics. What is Truman's schedule, where will he be and when. I won't have time to scout locations. Your local people will have to step in. You have people in Kansas City, right?"

"Yes."

According to the FBI, the Commies had people everywhere. "It'll have to be a public event, in the open. Or a parade, a motorcade, some site where I can take a shot from above. You understand?"

"That all makes sense, Alice."

"There's also the matter of the rifle. I'd prefer to use

mine, but it won't be possible. The gun will have to be hidden near the location. You have something to write on?"

"I have a good memory," Keller said. "Go ahead."

"I want a Springfield with a Weaver K10 scope attached. And don't forget the bullets. .30-06 M2 ball. 150 grain is fine."

"It'll take a few days for the affiliated union representatives to fill that order," he said.

"You have until Wednesday to organize the event. Meet me at the Double Play Bar. It's on 16th, like the last time, but walk east toward Franklin Park. Five o'clock. Bring your partner and the cash. I want half up front, ten grand, in hundreds, no bitching."

"I'll have the money."

"I figured you would. If you can't deliver the information and the rifle, the deal is off. Are we clear?"

"We'll deliver."

"Good. I also want a contact number in Kansas City. Bring it on Wednesday."

Vivian disconnected the call, wrote Keller's number on a notepad, and threw away the stained card. She could feel excitement building. She had been idle too long.

5. Monday Evening, April 28

Tom hadn't visited Pepper's Swing Club in months. Part of the reason was that too much over there reminded him of the horrors of the Forrester case. The gruesome hunt for the killer and the innocent girl who'd been stabbed—Maggie Bates who unexpectedly popped up on his horizon again. The job was another reason. He'd been busy. Crime never took a break. Then there was Rachel, and the gentle pressure of making their arrangement permanent. Another fallout of the Forrester assassination. He was hurt, and Rachel wasn't content to sit on the sidelines with her pad, taking notes. If she was going to worry about him, they might as well be married. You couldn't fault that line of reasoning. They were practically living together anyway. Tom's colleagues were betting on the color of his ties. The bachelor pretense was ridiculous.

He had to pop the question and Rachel had to answer. Stop the hesitation two-step, on both sides. The past months showed that they could be together and still do their respective jobs. It wouldn't be a *goodbye honey, see you at six with a pot roast* kind of marriage but neither of them was eager to go that boring route anyway.

After this Kansas City deal, once he'd proven to himself that he could handle the sultry Vivian Davis without tumbling into bed with her. The assignment promised to be demanding, in mind and matter.

Otis, Pepper's bartender, spotted him the moment he opened the door.

"Well, well, look what we got here. And without the sensational Rachel Holm. How come? She ditched you for a captain with golden epaulets and commendations?"

"I'm here on a job, Otis."

"What are you drinking? When we serve water, there's always something in it."

Tom ordered a scotch and soda. The club was busy; booths were occupied; the dance floor hopped; the music was bracing.

"It's nice to see that some things don't change."

"We do our best. If you've transferred to Vice, you're a bit early for serious action."

"I'm here to meet with a common friend. Looks like she's late."

Otis whistled. "Planets must be in a weird alignment. See Duke's poster over there on the left? There's a booth underneath with a *Reserved* board pinned on it. Go plonk yourself in there."

Tom took his drink and followed the instructions. It was quieter in that corner of the club, and discreet. If he put his back against the wall, he was a mere shadow on the paneling.

He didn't have long to wait, just enough time to finish his drink. Vivian slipped into the booth carrying a cocktail and a refill for his scotch.

"Is that hare-brained ploy of yours still on?" she said, without preamble.

She wore a clingy, silky, wine-colored dress with a puff of white lace that emphasized her cleavage more than it concealed it. Her dark hair was pulled to the side. It made her look exotic and went well with her perfume, a bit cloying, like a sweet tropical fruit drink.

He felt her foot brush his ankle and resisted changing position. "I told the feds I found a candidate. They want to meet you."

"For a measly one grand? No way."

"Come on, Vivian. They're not going to let you play in their big boys' game without asking a few questions."

She took a sip of her drink; it looked like a Tom Collins. "If you say I'm good, they should believe you. They don't trust you? You're too small-time for their taste?"

He knocked his glass against hers. "They're Hoover's worker bees. They don't take a leak without permission in triplicate. They wouldn't trust their brother if he wasn't a fed. And even then … Throw them a bone. Change your appearance. Wear something low-cut, make them blush, get them hot, and they'll be so preoccupied with what's happening in their underpants that they won't remember what you look like."

She laughed. "Are they boys or men, Tommy?"

"I guarantee they've never seen anything like you in the flesh, only on a screen."

"Not like you, eh? You've seen it all. Very mature."

"You got that right. Seriously now, you said you would be *invited* on the train."

"Abati booked a girl for the trip."

"Yes, I know. Pete Delgado is trying to find her address."

She smiled. "I know who she is and where she lives. She can be bought."

"It'll be safer to pick her up. Keep her out of circulation for the duration, with no opportunity to babble to anybody. I'll set it up with Pete. How does a deal like that work? Abati sends a car?"

"I'll have a conversation with her, girl to girl. Pete Delgado ... he's your partner?"

"The vice squad supervisor, and a friend." He grinned. "You'll like him."

"I don't hang around cops. It's not healthy."

"About that, where do you want to meet the feds? Not my office, obviously."

"Book a room at the Palace Hotel. Tomorrow. Leave the number with my answering service. I'll be there around ten. One flower in a big bouquet. There's no lack of girls hovering in these hotel corridors after the sun sets."

She lifted her glass in a playful toast.

6. Tuesday Evening, April 29

The sense of expectation in the hotel room was almost physical. Special agent Stansted appropriated the gilded chair by the vanity. He looked stiff and anxious, like a timid groom at his shotgun wedding. Burdon was more composed, sitting straight in an armchair upholstered in white brocade. Both feds had sniffled upon entering, taken aback by the surrounding luxury. Marble, thick carpets, a profusion of white and pink flowers in crystal vases, gilded sconces, and muslin drapes. Pete Delgado had reserved the bridal suite. *For a very special night,* he whispered in Tom's ear.

The feds got the joke. They didn't find it amusing. Worried about the bill, no doubt.

"We called in a favor with the hotel," Delgado said. "The flowers are from last night. The happy couple left them behind." He winked at Tom. "The bed's made fresh, and the bathroom is clean. In case it's needed."

"You have a dirty mind, Pete." The kind of thing you shouldn't say to a vice cop.

"Maybe the *Federales* will want to check the merchandise. Might do them good, they look constipated."

"Get out before I kick you where it hurts."

On his way to the door, Delgado pointed at the champagne chilling in a silver bucket. "Compliments of management." He clicked his heels and bowed.

The two FBI agents looked sour. Spinster sisters judging a bathing beauty contest.

Vivian was going to have a ball with these two. Tom looked forward to the show.

She didn't disappoint.

Tom took in the sights from the ground up. Red heels were strapped to her lovely ankles. Sheer nylons ran up and under a narrow black dress. How did she manage to put one foot in front of the other in that thing? Ah, there was a trick. She swayed thanks to a daring slit in the back that lined perfectly with her trim behind. A dark blue suede jacket sat just above her hips, pinched her waist with no apparent effort, and gaped to make room for her shapely chest. There was a thin slit there too, that revealed a sliver of smooth skin. Her hair was a warm auburn, pinned up to hold a flat hat, black with a red stripe that matched the shoes.

The effect was not entirely sophisticated. The dame could be had, but it would cost you. She was perfect. Delightful. Sinful. Tom refrained from clapping.

The two federal agents were gobsmacked.

Then she talked. Flat Midwest by way of Boston. It didn't matter. Nobody was checking provenance. "Lenora Grace, and you ah-r?"

Burdon jumped out of his armchair. "Uh, Special Agent Burdon." He didn't sound too sure he was that special. "This is my colleague, Stansted."

Stansted realized his mouth hung far too open and clapped it shut.

"Won't you have a glass of champagne, Miss Grace," Tom said. "Please have a seat."

She nodded at him and lowered herself onto the fluffy couch. The dress rode up revealing an enticing length of leg. Tom poured two glasses for the FBI guys. They looked like they needed a pick-me-up.

Burdon recovered first. "Did Detective Keegan explain what the job entails, Miss Grace?"

"Oh ya. Ya want me to cuddle da big mobstah."

Tom let out an involuntary chuckle that he drowned in champagne. She was overdoing it.

Burdon continued, undeterred. "We are looking for information."

"Sure. I get it. Tommy here didn't gild the lily, if you see what I mean." She winked.

The federal agent had a sudden fit of remorse. "It's dangerous, Miss Grace. We don't want you to get hurt."

She drained her champagne glass and held it out over the back of the sofa to Tom for a refill. "Well … either he talks, or he doesn't." She tilted her head, and the hat wobbled. "I know when to push and when to keep my trap shut. And Tommy said he'd have my back, so …" She smiled at Tom, with warm dewy eyes, full of pillowy promises.

"Yes, well." Burdon fidgeted in his chair. "Do you have questions, Miss Grace?"

"What about the dough?"

Tom focused on his champagne glass. Of course, she was going to bring it up. Vivian never gave up. She might even get away with it. Her legs made a stronger statement than whatever he could come up with.

"Didn't Detective Keegan go over the conditions?" Burdon said. His face was even more pinched than normal. How to talk money with a woman must not be part of his training. Her question also made obvious that they were paying her to have sex.

Agent Stansted, rigid on the gilded chair, had turned beet red. He stared at his shoes.

Vivian flashed a bright smile. "I prefer to conduct business with the top dog; it avoids misunderstandings."

She recrossed her legs and leaned forward on the sofa. Her back was to Tom and he didn't have the same view as Burdon, but it must have been a good one because the federal agent swallowed hard a couple of times. His Adam's apple bobbed above his stiff collar.

"I'll be with Abati nose to nose in a small sleeper," Vivian said. "It'll be sweaty work. And then there's Kansas City, for who knows how long." She drained her champagne glass. "Five thousand."

"I can't …" Burdon blurted.

Vivian put her glass on the coffee table. More fabric swishing. "Half before I get on the train, the rest on delivery. If I strike out, there's no charge." She made a regal hand wave. "Have the cash ready because I never strike out." There was a trace of smile in her voice.

"I have no doubt you're extremely competent." The words had trouble passing through Burdon's clenched teeth. "We can gather the, uh, advance fee. You will have expenses, I guess."

Fripperies, Tom thought. The contortions these guys went through, Jesus …

"If I may ask, Miss Grace," Burdon said. "How do you know Detective Keegan?"

Vivian turned on the sofa to glance at Tom. "A chance encounter. We helped each other."

She was being kind. She shot the man who was about to kill him. Tom didn't recall doing anything for her, except keeping her role in the Forrester case under wraps. Considering she'd been hired to take out Forrester, maybe his silence was worth something.

Burdon pushed himself out of his chair. "Well … we'll get things figured out, Miss Grace." He took a couple of hesitant steps toward the door. "We'll leave you to it. You can iron it out, right Keegan?"

Iron what? The black dress or the banknotes?

Burdon left the room, a wobbly Stansted on his tail. The door clicked close.

Tom stood with a champagne glass in his hand, amused at the feds' hasty retreat. He would have poked Vivian. How do you plan to seduce Abati, Miss Grace, do you have special tricks, a technique that never fails? He chuckled. He pictured Burdon straining to loosen his collar. He emptied his glass. He was being unfair, maybe Burdon and Stansted were decent guys who shied away from the ugly things their job made them do.

"Got steamy pretty quick, didn't it?" Vivian bent down and unstrapped her shoes, then she unpinned her hat and stretched full length on the couch. She popped the button that closed the jacket at her waist and let out a sigh of satisfaction. "I don't mind dressing up, but it feels good to release the gear." She raised herself on an elbow, looked at Tom. "Don't you think?"

He leaned on the credenza, the empty bottle of champagne behind him. "What do you think you're doing?"

"Takin' my time, sweet pea. I nailed the audition,

didn't I? They wanted to see me and they got what they came for." She looked around. "This is one posh room. Let's order room service on the FBI's dime. I wouldn't mind more of that excellent champagne."

Tom lit a cigarette and took a long leisurely look at the pleasant picture displayed on the sofa. She was a beautiful woman. What a shame to drop her in the lap of a pig like Mike Abati.

"Congratulations. I'm convinced you can disappear into a role, but how confident are you that you won't run into a goon you've had dealings with?"

She shrugged. "It isn't likely, and even if we've had a passing interaction, they won't recall. Females don't matter in that world. We're playthings discarded after the rut."

Tom was next to the sofa and hadn't realized he'd come to her. She grabbed his belt and pulled. She was strong and he came down on one knee, by her side. Her arms were around his neck and her warm mouth found his. He leaned into the kiss. The hand he didn't use to steady himself was around her waist, under the jacket. She was warm, soft, deliciously pliable.

"I like your weight on me," she muttered on the exhale.

It would be easy, so easy to give in ... He gave her another kiss, a light one, then gently disengaged and unlocked her arms. She didn't resist.

"You're impossible," she said.

*

Tom took the steps to his third-floor apartment two at a time, relieved the scene at the Palace Hotel ended as it did, with minimal damage. Pete Delgado thought he would throw the FBI agents for a spin, and he almost tripped his friend. *That* would get the office gamblers going a lot harder than a blue or green tie.

Impossible.

It was a relief to think so. If Vivian put up the barrier, Tom would only have to maintain it. She was like that last drink at the end of the party, the one you knew you would regret having in the morning but sounded damn good in the moment.

He briefly wondered if the tension that stretched between the two of them like the cable of a rope walker might go slack, deprived of energy, if he took her to bed. But that was wishful thinking. They were more alike than she knew. Single-minded and hungry for the chase. Maybe giving in to Vivian was a one-way trip that never reached its destination. Tom had no taste for the kind of sexual obsession that made for gripping reading. These tales never ended well.

He opened the apartment door. A light was on in the sitting room.

Rachel.

She was curled up on the sofa, wrapped in a plaid blanket, a discarded book in her lap. Tom couldn't remember what they'd decided the other night. *My place, your place?* With his irregular hours, planning was always a challenge. Her presence tonight was a sharp reminder of what was at stake. He wasn't single anymore. And he didn't want to be.

He dropped his hat and jacket in the hallway and went to the bathroom to check that Vivian hadn't left lipstick traces on his face or shirt. Amazing how duplicity came naturally to the males of the species—to the females too, probably. He made a face in the mirror. He wasn't cut for that kind of double game.

He sat on the edge of the davenport and kissed Rachel's cheek. She stirred and raised her arms in a sleepy embrace.

"How late is it?" she mumbled.

"Not yet midnight."

She wrinkled her nose. "You've been hanging around dancing girls?"

Almost. Rachel had keen investigative instincts. "The job took me to the bridal suite of a luxury hotel. There was no dead body, and it was rather pleasant. Unfortunately, I can't tell you what it was all about."

She sat up without removing her arms from his neck. "You realize cops always have the perfect cover story."

"I realize I'm lucky you're not the suspicious kind." He lifted her off the sofa and carried her to the bedroom. Then he went to the bathroom to take a shower.

*

In the morning, he made breakfast and brought the tray to her in bed. He knew Rachel would wonder why.

She hadn't forgotten the perfume from last night. "You really consorted with dancing girls if you need to make amends," she said.

"I didn't but I have to ask for forgiveness all the same. I have to go out of town. I might be away a week, and I can't tell you where I'll be."

"A homicide case?"

Tom shook his head. "I really can't tell you anything about it."

"Dangerous?"

"It shouldn't be. I'll call you, I promise. You just can't ask questions. I know it's hard. It goes against everything you are."

"The nosy, curious, relentless reporter. It's all right. Call it cop wife training. When are you leaving?"

Yes, he would pop the question after the Kansas City trip. He loved her. Wanted her. For the forever. Everything else was a distraction, as fleeting as mist over the Bay.

"I'm not sure. A day or two, I think. This whole thing is like shifting sands."

"Don't go adrift now, Tommy."

7. Wednesday Evening, April 30

Vivian stretched out on the woman's couch, her sturdy oxfords resting on a green throw pillow, automatic pistol in her lap. She'd had no trouble picking the apartment lock.

It was after midnight. Quiet. The telephone cord was cut. A reading lamp was on over her shoulder. She flipped through a recent issue of *Life* magazine. Marilyn Monroe beamed on the cover.

Two days ago, Vivian had visited the nondescript office of the area's top escort agency. She'd worked there for a short time after the war, before changing professions for good. For a C-note, the operator on duty told her that the girl hired by Abati for an upcoming weeklong rental was called Evelyn. No last name. No one cared about last names. Another ten dollars had delivered the girl's address. Idiots. Vivian never gave her address to the agency. There was no reason to be that forthcoming. Unless you accepted in-calls, which was neither smart nor safe.

Evelyn was out late.

Pete Delgado, the fast-talking, intense, and nicely dark-eyed vice supervisor—the San Francisco Police Department had a set of strapping gents—waited downstairs in an unmarked car with a tough-looking officer in a cheap suit. They dropped Vivian off outside the building and agreed to wait until three. She was more likely to get a call girl to cooperate than a couple of pushy cops. If Evelyn showed, the officers would come up after Vivian left. The girl would spend the next two weeks in jail on a prostitution charge, then let go for lack of evidence. It would keep her from running to Lima, eager for a reward.

The lock rattled and turned. Vivian set aside the magazine as Evelyn weaved into the room. She was clearly drunk on her impractical heels, and older than Vivian expected. Mid-thirties. She stopped when she saw Vivian on the sofa and reached for the support of a chair back.

"What the fuck?"

Vivian aimed the pistol at her.

"Who the fuck are you?"

Vivian placed an index finger on her lips.

"What the fuck do you want?"

"That's a lot of fucks," said Vivian. "Did you have a hard night?"

"Three men at a stag party. Jesus Christ. I need a break."

"I hear you, sister." Vivian patted the couch with the pistol. "Sit. Take a load off. You can have a nice long shower once we're done. First thing, though, tell me about your upcoming job with Abati."

"How do you know about the Abati job? And what's it to you?" Evelyn dropped on the opposite end of the couch, her red-rimmed eyes on the pistol.

"Because I want the job."

"You can have it. He's a pig."

"Why did you agree to it then?"

"He always asks for me." She shrugged.

"Why?"

"Because I'm old and a blonde and easily humiliated. He thinks I'm a pig like him. He thinks that stuff gets me horny. I don't know." Evelyn rubbed her arms, craving a hit. "Maybe I do like it."

"What did the agency tell you about the job?"

Evelyn wasn't pretty, but there was something sad about her that made her attractive. Maybe it was the eyes. Her body wasn't bad. Was she a crier? Some men liked to bring their girls to tears. It aroused them.

"A week out of town. Kansas City for fuck's sake. He was gonna pay me fifty a day. Cheapskate."

"Did he say why he was going to Kansas City?"

"I didn't talk to him. One of his gorillas called."

"You have your ticket? Assigned sleeping compartment?"

"Yeah. The agency sent it over. May I get up?"

Vivian gestured with the pistol. Evelyn went to a

secretary. She pulled an envelope out of a drawer and gave it to Vivian. "Ticket and berth."

Vivian got to her feet and handed Evelyn five hundred in cash. "Put this in a safe place as soon as I shut the door behind me."

"Gee, thanks."

"What's Abati into?"

"In the sack? He's a pig. Like I said."

"Meaning what?"

"He likes handcuffs. And he's always at my ass with that stubby cock of his."

Vivian felt a wave of disgust. Handcuffs bruised her wrists, and she had no taste for backdoor boondoggles.

8. Friday, May 2

"Maggie!"

Vivian carried her heavy suitcase to the living room and set it by the door. A cab was on its way. She wore a tight blue dress that came to her knees, new stockings, stylish underwear, and heels. The oxfords were packed in the hard case, along with an assortment of dresses, sweaters, and her makeup kit. No weapons.

"Maggie!"

The girl came out of her bedroom with a toothbrush in her mouth.

"Have you seen my handcuffs?"

Maggie nodded and raced to the kitchen to spit in the sink. She drank water from her cupped hand, swished it around in her mouth, and spit again before wiping her lips on a tea towel. All the while Vivian tapped her foot.

"They're in the junk drawer," said Maggie.

"Would you bring them to me, please?"

Maggie pulled open the drawer next to the sink, set a wrench, a flick-knife, a .22 pistol with silencer attached, and a ball of rubber bands onto the counter. She lifted out the handcuffs. The key was inserted into the lock. She carried them to Vivian, who dropped the jangly apparatus into her purse.

"Does this trip involve you taking yourself to jail?" asked Maggie.

"You're funny this morning."

"Where are you going? If I may ask."

"I told you that I'm not supposed to tell anyone." Vivian flicked through her purse, double-checking the departure time on her ticket, then looked up when the girl began to play something on the piano. A bouncy bluesy thing. She sang a couple of verses.

"What's that?" Vivian's nerves started to prickle.

"Something I heard recently on the Federal label."

"Am I supposed to care?"

"It's Little Willie on piano. Of course you should care.

Do you want to know what it's called?" Maggie smirked.

"I want to get out of here. Okay, what's it called?"

"*Kansas City.*"

"That will do." Vivian closed the keyboard cover on Maggie's fingers.

"Ouch. You shouldn't have left the ticket on your dresser."

"You shouldn't be snooping in my bedroom."

"I was worried. What if something happens to you? What will happen to me if you don't come back?"

"You'll be rich." The ten grand from the Commies had been added to her safe, along with the twenty-five hundred from the feds. "The combination to the closet safe is written on the underside of the junk drawer. There's a lot of cash in there. Jewelry, too. Enough to put you through school at a fancy conservatory. It'll keep you living here for as long as you want. And nothing is going to happen to me."

Maggie hopped off the piano bench and embraced Vivian.

"Tell me about your trip." Maggie had never left the city in the seven years since her arrival from the Philippines.

"Sacramento. Then Reno. Salt Lake. I change trains in Cheyenne. Head to Denver, then on to Kansas City."

"Wow," said Maggie. "All those big cities. What an adventure."

"I've never been to any of those places. Except Sacramento." That was years ago, for a contract hit. A minor politician she gunned down from a hotel window. Easy as peach pie. The thought gave her pause. She dug in her purse again and pulled out a small address book. "Give me a pen and a piece of paper." She copied a telephone number. "In case of emergency. Ask for Pete Delgado."

"Okay," Maggie said. "Be careful."

"I'm always careful, kid."

*

Tom took a cab to the Southern Pacific Railroad Station on Third Street. He didn't want to be seen arriving with anybody who looked like a cop. His blue suit was subdued, a mid-price number that matched what half the men wore, except for the smart cut that hid the shoulder holster with his service Colt. His leather suitcase was sturdy and scuffed, pegging him as a frequent traveler. He shot an appreciative glance at the Mission style train depot, its elegant arcades and wide marquee. He held the door open for a woman and stepped into the vast waiting room with its long wooden benches. He went straight to the platform, not needing to stop at the ticket office. Pete Delgado had done well and found him a compartment in the next car over from Vivian's.

He saw the two dark suits surrounding Mike Abati right away, broad shoulders, bulky shapes. The muscle. He didn't have to walk past them to reach his reserved seat. There was no sign of Vivian yet. This was according to plan. He was supposed to be on board before her.

Fifteen minutes to departure.

*

The taxicab dropped Vivian at the corner of Third and Townsend. *Southern Pacific* in large block letters was squeezed between two red-tiled eaves over the arched front entrance of the station. She lugged her suitcase into the waiting room and showed her ticket to a porter who directed her to the proper track. The train left a little before noon.

Abati stood next to the train, thick body in a dark suit, his salt-and-pepper hair combed straight back from his forehead. Vivian imagined what all that oil would feel like. She swallowed her distaste and brought her mind back to the job. A large thug stood on either side of Abati, one looking to the front, one to the back. They both wore fedoras. She recognized Leo, the Nutcracker, from the picture Pete Delgado showed her during a briefing session with Tom Keegan at Pepper's the evening before. The FBI agents weren't in attendance. After the meeting at the Palace Hotel, they weren't going to conduct business at a jazz club. Delgado had been entrusted with the money. Her two detectives, Vivian mused. They made quite a pair. If they'd taken her for a spin on the dance floor, the evening would have been perfect, but they were both too serious. As serious as the two Commies she'd sat down with. Men and their work ethic ...

Like that Nutcracker guy. One who enjoyed his job too. *Be careful around him,* Delgado had said. *He's a pervert and a sadist.* The other bodyguard was younger. Athletic and baby-faced, which didn't make him less dangerous. He wasn't in Delgado's photo collection. The husky boy watched her approach and pursed his lips for a whistle that he didn't complete when she dropped her suitcase in front of Abati.

She'd gotten there just in time; people were boarding the train all around her. Being late was the only way to play this.

"Can I help you?" said Abati.

"Are you Mike? The agency sent me. Evelyn broke her ankle when some shit-faced mug threw her down the stairs in a fit of pleasure. I'm her replacement. Sorry for the short notice."

"Leo," said Abati. "Call the agency. See if her story checks out."

"We don't got time, boss," said the baby-faced thug.

The train started to make hisses of departure.

"All aboard!" yelled a man in a cap and smart uniform as he walked past.

Abati motioned for the entourage to follow him. They went around the rear of the train, up the other side of it, and through a door into a dark hallway. The door led to the street. They came out into sunshine. A cab waited at a stand on the corner. Abati tapped on the roof to alert the driver that he had a fare. The goons opened the doors for Abati and Vivian. They seemed surprised by the turn of events. The young one put the suitcases in the trunk.

"What's the deal, boss?" Leo said.

"I always ask for a blonde."

Vivian felt nervous perspiration in her armpits. The job wasn't ten minutes old, and it was already going sideways. She couldn't warn Tom. Wherever he was. She was soon pressed against Abati when the men packed inside the cab.

"If I wanted to wallow in black-haired bush, I'd bring my niece over from Monte San Giuliano." Abati's cologne made Vivian's eyes water. "I ordered my regular blonde. This one shows up. A black swan. Something ain't right. *Non mi va.*" He shook his head.

"I'll make sure you have a good time." Vivian jiggled her bag. The handcuffs rattled.

"Look in the purse," Abati said to Leo. "Handcuffs? She could be a cop. Make sure that's the most interesting thing she's got in there."

The man dug around in the bag as the cab sped away. "She's clean."

"I hope so," Abati said.

Soon they were crossing the velvety blue bay on the long bridge to Oakland. Vivian wondered if Tom had noticed she wasn't on the train. If these goons managed to get to a phone, she was in for a rough time. She couldn't fight her way past them with no weapon. She grew anxious as the cab bounced along and wished she'd let Maggie know the name of the garage where she kept her Studebaker Roadster. It was nearly new. The key was in the kitchen junk drawer. The girl could sell the car and make a bundle.

After twenty minutes, the overcrowded taxi pulled behind a building in a neglected part of downtown Oakland. Abati and his boys hustled Vivian inside through a rusted iron door. She carried her suitcase. The place was a nightclub or a gambling den, dark and empty at noon, although the kitchen was up and running. Vivian noted the bar, scattered card tables, and low stage.

Abati pushed her up the stairs next to the bar to a bedroom on the second floor. He closed the door for privacy and dropped his pants. The message was clear. Vivian got on her knees, hoping her stockings didn't tear, and made quick work of him with her mouth. After he emptied, he held her chin in his hand and looked down into her dark eyes. Her lipstick must be smeared into a clown's grin. She wasn't grinning.

"That was an expert job, glamour-puss. What should I call you this week when I need you for a bit of fun, you must have a working name, Princess, maybe?"

"Queen is what my men call me. When they're on *their* knees."

Vivian wanted to spit. In his face. It would take four glasses of wine at least to wash the taste of him out of her mouth.

Abati returned his pants to his waist, tucked in his shirt, and brought the belt together.

"King and Queen on the prowl. This is gonna be some vacation, sweetheart." He yanked up the zipper. "Queenie. Get yourself straightened up and come down for lunch."

Abati opened the door.

"Should I call the agency like you said?" asked Leo who'd been standing guard outside.

"Nah. She's no cop. But keep an eye on her. And go through her suitcase."

The room had a full bathroom. Must be one of Abati's hideouts. Vivian gargled and realigned her lipstick while Leo went through her things. She'd gotten the program back on track. But where was the track going? She shut off the bathroom light and walked down the stairs to the main room, the guard on her tail.

Abati and the young thug were seated at a table. Both had beers in front of them.

"Sit Queenie," said Abati. "Order some pasta. You could use a little meat on those hips."

"My ass is soft enough." She sat on a hard chair.

"We'll find out."

"Can I get a salad here? And a glass of burgundy wine?"

"Oooh. A high-class dame, boss."

"Shut up, Aldo."

The kid needed a shave. Leo, the broad-shouldered thug with graying temples and a sagging jowl, ordered her salad and wine at the bar.

"What's his name?" Vivian nodded at the wide back.

"That's Leo. He's my tough guy. Don't get sassy with him."

"Ain't I tough, boss?"

"Yeah, Aldo, but he's got brains."

Pete Delgado had warned her. Leo was the one to watch. Vivian took a swallow of the wine he brought her. It was surprisingly good. She set the glass down and pulled her chair up to the table. She was ready to play now that she had regained a measure of control.

"What's going on? We're not taking the train anymore? I don't mind a road trip, but I like to know where I'm headed."

Abati grabbed her hand and put it in his crotch. "You know where you're headed."

The two goons thought that was the funniest thing their boss ever said, and guffawed. Vivian gave Abati a little squeeze and immediately regretted it. It looked like he might be ready to go again. The man must not get what he needed at home.

"My sister thinks I'm headed to KC. A girl's gotta make sure another girl always knows where she is in this racket. Plenty of bad turns out there. Can I call her and tell her where I'm going?"

Abati snorted. "Kansas City is still on. Something felt off at the station. I got my instincts, babe." He tapped the side of his nose. "When it don't smell right, I swing left."

Abati was lucky Vivian hadn't been hired to take him out, he'd be dead meat on the platform.

"We'll sit tight and take the night train down to L.A."

She whistled. "The Oakland Lark? That's an all-Pullman run. I know that train. It's packed to the gills with movie stars and businessmen. Diamond-studded. Can't get a cabin on short notice."

"She don't know much, does she boss?"

"Shut up, Aldo. Use your noodle. How could she possibly know?" Abati laughed.

"You have a standing reservation," said Vivian.

"Hey, the broad got brains!" Abati knocked his big fist against Vivian's head. "We'll get to Kansas City, babe. No worries."

"KC. Jesus. What can a girl do in Kansas City for a week?"

He leaned toward her, a leer on his broad face. "If you play your cards right, treat me like a king, maybe I'll let you do some shopping. We'll get us some Kansas barbecue. They got red hot jazz clubs. And plenty of booze." He grabbed her shoulder. Dug his thick fingers in. "In case I'm not enough for you, *cara*. Which I doubt." He laughed again and the goons laughed in concert.

"Okay if I go upstairs and take a nap?" Vivian yawned. "Wine makes me a little dopey."

"Sure," said Abati. "Get your beauty rest. Aldo? Take your chair up and sit outside the door. I don't want anyone bothering my Queenie."

They trudged up to the room. Vivian closed the door and heard the legs of Aldo's chair scrape on the worn wood flooring of the hallway. He was blocking the door.

She looked out the window. There was a phone booth on the street corner, but no fire escape to get down there. She might break a leg dropping from the second floor, and if she pulled it off, how would she get back up? She raised the blinds and jerked up the window. If Aldo poked his head in, she'd tell him she needed to get some air. There was no easy way down, but a drainpipe rose up to the roof, right above her head. She leaned out to study it. From the pipe to the roof, and then what? There might be an access of some sort.

She took a couple of dimes from her purse and looked for her address book. Handcuffs, compact, lipstick, hankie, hairpins. No address book. She had taken it out to give Pete Delgado's number to Maggie. Did Leo snatch it when he searched her things? No, she would have seen him give it to Abati. She must have left the thing at the apartment. Damn. She should have memorized Delgado's number, like she did for the Kansas City contact the Reds gave her. Because these guys told her she couldn't write anything down.

She had to call Maggie at the apartment.

She went to the window and took hold of the pipe. Soon she was pulling herself over the parapet. Even before she got her hips over the edge of the roof, she could see the curled rail of a ladder at the back of the building. She'd torn her stockings. She took off her heels and left them on the roof. She hurried down the ladder in tattered nylon. The back alley stank with overflowing garbage cans. A piece of gravel dug into her heel and she hopped, cursing.

When she reached the sidewalk, she strolled casually to the phone booth. She dropped in a dime, and dialed Maggie at the apartment.

She hoped the girl was still home. She wished she remembered a good prayer.

"Hello," came the tinny voice.

"Maggie. It's Viv. You've got to call Pete Delgado. I wrote down the number for you, remember? Tell him Abati got jumpy at the station and nixed the ride at the last moment. I'm holed up with him and his boys in Oakland and we're planning to leave for L.A. on the overnight Lark at around nine. We're still headed to KC, so Delgado doesn't need to do anything except spread the word."

"Who's Abati?"

"Just call Delgado. Quick." Vivian slammed down the handset.

She exited the booth and ran across the street, through the alley, and up the ladder. She dashed to the parapet, strapped on the heels, and lowered herself down the drainpipe.

When she reached for the windowsill, her foot slipped. She grabbed the edge with both hands. She looked down. Leo was on the sidewalk, smoking a cigarette. She hung there, concentrating on the loose shoe that threatened to fall off. She was glad she still trained with barbells at the City College gymnasium a few nights a week.

Just as the muscles in her arms began to burn, Leo

finished his cigarette. He flicked it into the street and went back inside. Vivian crawled up and over the sill. She dropped onto the floor with a clunk, her arms trembling. She went to the door and listened. Aldo was snoring. She ripped off her stockings and removed her soot-covered dress. She rolled it into a ball, slipped it into her laundry bag, and opened the spigots over the tub.

She soaked for a long while, then removed a green dress and a fresh pair of stockings from her suitcase. Aldo was sound asleep when she opened the door. He was tilted back in the chair. Balanced just so. She kicked the supporting legs and sent him sprawling. He rolled around and got to his feet, groping for his gun, alarmed.

"Sorry, kid. Take me to our leader."

Abati, Leo, and a couple of thugs were playing cards in an island of bright light. Vivian dragged a chair a few feet behind Leo and sat as prettily as she could with her legs spread, fanning the skirt over her knees. The men found it hard to contain their stares. Abati started winning.

They all ate when the game ended. Vivian downed three glasses of wine and wondered if her message had gotten to Tom Keegan.

The Oakland Lark left from the 16th Street Station at nine p.m. It was a twelve-hour ride to Los Angeles.

*

Tom waited half an hour before going to check on Abati and his crew. He figured the bodyguards would be standing outside the compartment. With a bit of luck, he could peek in and catch a glimpse of Vivian. He wanted her to see him.

He crossed over from his car to the next. Three men were in the corridor, smoking, none of them were Abati's gorillas. They must all be inside the compartment. He hoped the curtains weren't drawn close.

The curtains were open, but the compartment was empty, no suitcases in the luggage rack.

Twenty minutes later, Tom had walked the entire length of the train twice. Mike Abati and Vivian were not onboard. Rescuing Special Agent Burdon's plan was going to require improvisation, something the FBI was not designed to excel at.

First stop Sacramento. For one hour and a half Tom bit his nails to the quick.

He was by the door with his suitcase, ready to jump as soon as the train came to a stop.

He ran down the platform.

Find a goddamn phone. Three booths, all occupied. Two women, one burly guy who gesticulated in the small space. Pretty worked up. Tom knocked on the door. He held up his badge. The man opened the door. He screamed in the phone, "hold on a minute."

To Tom: "Whaddya want?"

"Police business. I need the phone, sir."

"Yeah? Wait your fucking turn, buddy." He went to close the door, but Tom's foot was already in there. "God damn it, can't you see I'm in the middle of something?" The guy's face was flushed to begin with, now he was turning purple. He yanked at the door handle.

Tom took the Colt out of the shoulder holster. "It's loaded. Get the fuck out."

The man's eyes went wide. "You wouldn't ..."

"Emergency. I asked politely. Now haul your ass out of there."

The man dropped the phone and exited the box. "You're crazy. I'm getting the cops."

Tom ignored him. He picked up the phone, said, "he'll call you back," and cut the communication.

The phone rang twice before Pete Delgado picked up.

"They're not on the train. I'm in Sacramento."

"I expected your call, Tommy. Maggie Bates just called. Vivian called her from Oakland. Abati got the willies and didn't board the train. He's taking the Lark tonight to L.A., and to Kansas City from there. The end game remains the same."

"Except I'm nowhere near Vivian. How did she

manage to slip away?"

"Don't know. Maggie said she was in a hurry and didn't answer her questions."

Tom let out a curse. "What do I do now? My train's gone. I might as well come back and catch the Lark in Oakland. What does Burdon suggest?"

Delgado chuckled. "He's run out of ideas. The man is a master planner."

Somebody banged on the door. Tom turned around and saw a uniformed cop pointing a gun at him. The flustered guy was behind the policeman.

"Jesus. Hold on, Pete. I have a situation here." Tom slapped his badge against the glass. The cop squinted and took a couple steps back. He put his gun away. "Pete? I'll get back to you after I have a look at the train options. Maybe I can get to Kansas City ahead of Vivian and be in position near the Mob meeting instead of trying to catch up with her."

"You're not coming back here?"

"She's with Abati and his crew. If her cover was blown, he wouldn't take her to L.A. Put one of your guys on the Lark, so we don't lose contact. The FBI can give you a couple of agents in Los Angeles, to make sure Abati and company board the train down there. Have one on the KC train, if that doesn't blow their budget. We're reshuffling the deck. Is Burdon nearby? Or Stansted?"

He heard Delgado call Burdon, who came on the phone.

"How do I make contact with the FBI in Kansas City?" Tom said.

"We'll have agents at Union Station," Burdon said, "as planned."

"I won't be on the train they expect, and Mike Abati won't be either. Unless my contacts have set up permanent residence at the station, they won't be there when I come in. Your people are monitoring the mobsters' arrivals. Where's your command post?"

Burdon took a long time to answer. "The Jackson

County Court House, at Twelfth and Oak." He sounded reluctant.

"Who's in charge?"

Another agonized pause. You needed pliers to get words out of the guy.

"Special Agent Thorpe."

"Okay, I'll be in touch." Tom hung up and stepped out of the phone booth.

The Sacramento cop waited, both fists on his hips. "This is highly irregular."

Tom pointed at the red-faced guy he ejected from the phone booth. "I told this gentleman it was an emergency, police business, and showed him the badge. He refused to vacate the box. That's obstruction. I didn't want to use physical force, and I was in a hurry, so I showed him my service weapon."

The cop turned to the civilian. "Refusing to comply is an offense, sir. Detective Keegan is an officer of the law. What do you want me to do, Mr. Keegan?"

"I'm done. He can have the phone." Tom searched his pockets and extracted a dime. He gave it to the cop. "That should do, right?"

*

Telling Pete Delgado and Burdon that he would try to make it to Kansas City before Abati was all well and fine, but Tom had no idea how to do it. He could wait for the next train out of Sacramento and catch a connection in Cheyenne. He needed timetables to figure out if it would get him to Missouri ahead or behind the mobster and his entourage.

Another option, the easiest, was to forget about beating Abati to KC, hop on a train back to San Francisco, then take the Lark from Oakland to L.A. He would not sleep much, that train was always fully booked, but he would be near Vivian.

Tom grabbed his suitcase and looked for the ticket office. He hoped the attendant had a stack of train schedules because finding the best route would take some juggling.

The waiting room was a lot busier than when he

arrived. The noise emanated from a cheerful group of airmen.

Tom paused. The Air Force? Wild idea ... worth a try.

He grabbed one of the young men by a sleeve. He flashed his badge. "Where are you based?"

The kid stared at him. "Mather, why?"

"That's around here?"

"Ten miles east of town."

"You have planes?"

The kid laughed. "We better. Navigation school. Not much use if you stay on the ground."

Tom hailed a cab in front of the train station.

*

Convincing security at the gate to let him through was easy, Tom's badge was seeing a lot of action today. Explaining why he needed a plane ride to Kansas City was a challenge. One of the nifty FBI cards Special Agent Burdon waved around would have come handy.

The captain who agreed to see him, after the sergeant in the outer office gave up trying to understand what he was asking for, was friendly and baffled.

"I have the utmost respect for your wartime service, Keegan, and I believe you're a serious man doing an important job, but why the hell would I give you a plane for a cross-country hop?"

"You could make it a navigation exercise. From Sacramento to Kansas City by the shortest route, challenging relief, possible weather."

The captain grinned. "I know the trainees who would benefit. Still ... You have to give me something, Keegan. We have forms to fill in, you know."

"All it'll take is a phone call." Tom rattled off Pete Delgado's number. "Let me talk first."

The captain went along. He was amused, and curious.

"Give me Burdon again," Tom said, as soon as Pete picked up. To the Air Force captain: "Special Agent Burdon from the FBI is in charge. He can tell you things that I'm not at liberty to divulge." When Burdon came on the line, Tom told him where he was. "Explain to the captain why I need to go to Kansas City, Burdon." He gave the phone to the captain and lit a cigarette. It was his turn to be amused.

The captain listened, made approbative sounds, grunted a couple of times, managed to put in a couple words sideways, "there are trains." Burdon must have nipped that objection in the bud—which Tom appreciated; he didn't expect the FBI agent to come through for him—because the captain said, "I understand," and hung up.

"Quite a story," he said, when the phone was back in the cradle. "And you don't know what's going on?"

"That's the whole point. We want to find out."

"It could have national security implications."

Tom nodded. "Hoover is an earnest man." He thought that was debatable but swallowed his sarcasm.

The captain stepped from behind the desk and straightened his uniform. "Let's get the show on the road. Don't expect a padded seat and a smiling stewardess. Our training crates are stripped down."

9. Saturday, May 3

Abati crawled out of his bunk at a stop called Guadalupe. The conductor woke everyone at dawn with his bellowing from the platform. Vivian emerged from the warm blankets and hung her messy tresses over the edge of the upper-bunk railing. Abati dressed quickly and zipped a comb through his oily hair.

"Can I stay under the covers a bit longer? You wore me out last night."

"Get dressed, Queenie. Show off that fine frame of yours. I'll be in the dining car. A hearty breakfast will bring your energy back."

"Okey-doke."

Abati had claimed the bottom bunk when they got to the cabin the night before. He ordered her to join him in the narrow space and rode her from behind. He pointed at the ladder when he was finished. She'd been happy to climb away from him. The boys, Leo and Aldo, were nowhere to be seen during the night, probably taking turns dozing in the lounge car and standing outside the compartment door. She needed a bath. She felt unclean and wondered how many more times she'd be asked to perform before she could give herself a good scrub.

She stepped into yesterday's wrinkled dress, brushed her hair, rinsed her face at a tiny sink, and attempted to apply fresh lipstick as the train lurched side to side.

She entered the dining car on trembling heels after passing through four jerking Pullmans. Abati waved her over to the table where he hovered over a colossal plate of greasy food. She sat in the chair opposite him, squirming on her sore bottom. Abati noticed her grimace and laughed out loud. Heads turned to enjoy the joke. She wasn't smiling. Van Johnson sat at the table across the aisle from them. Still cute in his blond, athletic way. He appeared to be trying to remember if he'd seen her somewhere. He wouldn't remember. Vivian winked at him. The woman across from him glared.

A Negro came to take Vivian's order, and she decided

to humor Abati by asking for the Special Club Breakfast—orange juice, griddle cakes, sausage, and coffee. What she needed more than anything was coffee. Abati beamed at the impending return of her carnal energy.

"So, what's the plan for today?" Vivian spread a napkin out on her lap.

"We'll arrive in Los Angeles at nine or so, then change to the Kansas City train. We'll spend one more night on wheels and arrive around noon. There's a big bed waiting for us at The Elms in Excelsior Springs."

Vivian tried her best to look enthusiastic. "Is that in Kansas City?"

"Nearby. It's a resort. There's a spa, swimming pool, tennis, golf. Enough to do to keep the gathered parties from wandering off to drinking establishments, gambling halls, and whorehouses between meetings."

"Is everyone bringing a whorehouse with them?"

"You're not the only girl along for the ride. You can enjoy the steaming waters all together."

"I didn't bring a bathing suit."

"We'll get you one. I bet they sell them at the hotel. The place is swanky."

"Is there a theme to this gathering?" She yawned. "What are you all jabbering about?"

The question had been too direct, and his face turned hard. "None of your business, Queenie."

The car went dark. Wall sconces popped to dim life. Vivian spread the venetian blinds with her fingers. She saw nothing but blackness. "What the hell just happened?"

"The Santa Susana tunnel. Gave you the shivers, huh?" Abati chuckled.

"Oh, I'm not afraid of the dark. Just surprised me is all." Her coffee arrived.

"You're cute. It won't be long before we get in." He picked up a newspaper.

Vivian's food was delivered a minute later, and she pecked at it while the train rolled through Simi Valley, North

Hollywood, and tooted into sprawling Union Station. She and Abati returned to the cabin for their things and were joined in the corridor by Aldo and Leo.

They stepped off the train and moved under shady awnings toward the inner workings of the booming station.

"Hustle on to ticketing, Leo, and grab us four to Kansas City," said Abati. "You won't be able to snare us a cabin this late in the game. We'll have to sit up all night. Queenie can rest her pretty head on my shoulder while I stroke her knee."

The goons chuckled. Vivian was happy to hear her caboose would get the night off.

"May I freshen up?"

"Sure, baby. Aldo's gonna walk you to the bathroom."

"I'm a big girl. I can walk there all by myself."

"Don't talk back. Aldo, look after her."

The young man walked at her side and they followed the signs to the bathrooms. He basked in the envious looks he got from passing men. Vivian straightened his tie and left him outside the ladies' entrance with her suitcase. She had enough tools in her purse to make up her face. She hurried to the window to see if she could spot a pay telephone. She wanted to try Maggie again, to find out if word of her change in direction had gotten to Tom. No luck. The windows were barred.

As she and Aldo walked back, a man whistled at her. Aldo took the challenge personally and turned to grab the man's arm. He dropped her suitcase, ready to clobber the whistler. Vivian pulled him back.

"Honey. Baby." She kissed his cheek. "It's not worth it. Let that mug wonder what I look like on top of you in bed." Aldo's jaw dropped and the interloper hurried away. She picked up her suitcase. "Keep moving, kid. Come on. You can buy me some magazines. It's going to be a long ride. And wipe that lipstick off your face. The boss is waiting. Let's go. On the double."

Aldo stood stunned. She took his elbow to get him going.

Two hours later, they settled onto two facing benches on the eastbound *Super Chief.*

*

Every time she opened her eyes in the rocking train car, Vivian felt a chill. Leo, seated directly across from her, was undressing her with his big brown half-lidded eyes. Aldo slept next to him on the bench seat with his fedora pulled down to his nose, his arms crossed over his chest. Vivian was against the outer wall of the train car. Moonlight glazed the distant mountains.

"Try to leave me something to wear, big boy."

"You can't expect me to control my eyes. It's biology."

Abati grumbled. "Leo. Knock it off. You're making Queenie uncomfortable. Switch seats with Aldo. Give the girl a break."

Leo curled his lips and shook Aldo's shoulder. The kid opened his eyes in a panic. He pulled a revolver from a shoulder holster. Leo slapped his arm down. Abati turned red. Vivian glanced around at the sleeping riders, shook her head, and sighed. If she was nabbed after the Truman job, spending the rest of her life in prison surrounded by women didn't sound bad at all.

*

The plane ride was a hard one. When they landed at Grandview Airport, south of Kansas City, Tom was stiff and crampy. He was also wired after all the coffee he'd ingested to keep warm, and he badly needed to take a leak. The pilot and student navigators wore padded leather jackets. His thin suit made him long for his wartime uniform. That wool was a lot warmer.

Grandview Airport was being turned into an Air Force Base and a steady stream of trucks brought in construction workers and materials. Tom hitched a ride into town that was as bumpy and hard on his tailbone as the plane trip. He wasn't complaining, things were coming together better than expected.

The Jackson County Court House was a massive pile of Art Deco concrete, thirteen floors of offices, courtrooms, and jails. Everybody in there was in a state midway between frenzy and panic. Nobody had a second to spare to point Tom in the right direction.

He must have walked a couple of miles, lugging his suitcase, before he found the section of floor commandeered by the FBI team in charge of the Mob gathering.

Special Agent Thorpe was agitated. He was in his shirtsleeves, tie undone, yelling in a phone when he took a break from yelling at his scurrying troops. Tom was familiar with emergencies in the squad room but such a level of chaos he had never seen. At least two dozen agents were running around, their purpose unclear. Four women sat at a long table, answering calls. A large map of Kansas City and surrounding localities occupied half a wall. Pictures of swarthy-looking men were pinned on cardboard panels. To Tom's tired eyes, they all looked the same.

He dropped his suitcase on an empty chair and pushed his badge in Thorpe's face.

"Keegan, SFPD. I'm on the Mike Abati detail."

Thorpe stopped yelling in the phone to bark at Tom. "Abati's arrived?"

"He got squirrelly and changed trains. He'll be here tomorrow, on the *Super Chief* from Los Angeles."

Thorpe squinted. "Good to know. Who's with him?"

"A notorious tough, Leo Barbieri, also known as the Nutcracker, and a kid. Don't know him, he's not on file."

Thorpe scribbled the information on a piece of paper. "Hopefully Abati will stay on script and join the others at The Elms. Keeping an eye on these goons in the wild is a nightmare."

"My girl is with him," Tom said.

"That play is over. She's no longer needed." Thorpe grabbed the handset to resume his shouting match.

Tom put his hand on the phone. "Excuse me?"

Thorpe must have seen something in Tom's eyes because he made a placating gesture. "You know it was always a sideshow, right? Informants are coming out of the woodwork with gossip about a hit on the President. We're dealing with more than fifty Mob gunslingers in town, thousands of rodeo visitors, suspects left and right. Half the country hates Truman's guts. I don't have time for a little hooker and whatever she can extract from a low-level mobster. Do us a favor, Keegan. Retrieve the girl and take her back home. It'll be one less thing to worry about."

Tom pointed at the pictures on the board. "It's an assassin with a sniper rifle you should worry about, not these mugs."

"You think I don't know that?"

There was no mistaking the bitter anger in Thorpe's voice. The man was a professional hamstrung by bureaucratic stupidity.

"I'm sorry," Tom said. "I'll take care of the girl."

A girl who could teach J. Edgar Hoover a thing or two about killers-for-hire. It was a good thing Vivian was defanged and declawed or she'd be a prime suspect. And Tom better haul her out of town before she got caught in the FBI sweep.

He picked up his suitcase and left.

*

Tom found a room in a hotel three blocks from the train station. The place was bare bones, but the closet-size room was clean and the lobby bar was decent, which helped because he doubted he would manage to catch more than a few winks.

He felt guilty about Vivian. Not only did he put her in Abati's clutches, but she'd been humiliated and degraded for nothing. Tomorrow, he would have to tell her the FBI scuttled the assignment because they had their hands full with Truman. She would despise him and put him in the same box as Abati and all the men who had taken advantage of her.

Three double whiskeys and a dry excuse for a sandwich that sat on his empty stomach like a chunk of concrete didn't do a lick to improve his mood. When he caught his reflection in the bar mirror, he decided he'd better go to bed. He looked too much like the two hammered salesmen swaying on their stools next to him. If he stayed any longer, they would think he was one of them and buy him a drink, setting up a destructive self-pitying spiral. He didn't need that kind of misery.

A long shower and turning down the lights helped bring the situation into perspective. In a few more hours the misguided operation would be over. Then he could look forward to a two-day train trip with Vivian who would tell him to go to hell and take the entire FBI with him.

It was stifling in the small room and he opened a window. Street traffic had dwindled to a trickle. The street was quiet. He heard a church bell ring once nearby. With the time difference it wasn't too late to call California. Not to report on the aborted mission. FBI agents Burdon and Stansted could wait for a complete rundown until Vivian was safe. He was sure they didn't give a damn.

Tom called the operator and gave her Rachel's number. Two rings and she picked up.

"I'm in a gloomy hotel room staring at the ceiling," he said.

"In a town that will remain nameless. You sound tired."

"I am. And irritated out of my skin at myself and the entire police business. Stop me if I run at the mouth. I feel a furious urge to rant."

"I wish I was there to witness it," Rachel said. "I've long wondered what hid behind your stoic demeanor. It's all right to lose your temper, you know. Occasionally. It's healthy to let out steam."

He laughed. "Stoic, my foot. Ask Al Matteotti what happens when a case goes sideways."

"Is this one getting lost in the weeds?"

"If only I had weeds to whack." Tom sighed. "It was a dumb plan from the start and I should have kept my mouth shut. Let the whole thing go to pot instead of trying to make it work."

"And you're still trying to fix it, is that it?"

"It's over. Which is why I'm flat on my back, watching

streetlights dance on the ceiling, having bitter thoughts. I need your soft voice and a helping hand to lift me out of a damn puddle of the blues. I also want a cigarette, but you hate it when I smoke in bed, so I'll refrain. And I miss you."

Silence. Rachel didn't believe in the automatic serve-return of love speak. If she replied with 'I miss you too', it meant she was distracted and not listening.

"I hate not knowing where you are," she said. "Does that make me possessive?"

He chuckled. "I'll tell you everything when I'm back home. Off the record. And you'll call me an idiot."

She sighed. "I love you, Tommy. When will you be home?"

"I might be underway tomorrow. I'll call as soon as I know for sure. Rachel?"

"Yes."

"For a fast-talking reporter, you listen better than anybody I know."

"You have a voice for radio. I close my eyes and I swoon."

He could hear the smile behind her words. "Good night, babe. I love you."

10. Sunday, May 4

"Hey glamour pants." Leo was giving Vivian the shit again. "Let's head up to the Pleasure Dome."

She turned to look at him. Abati was in the bathroom where he spent a good deal of his time. Constipated. Aldo must be standing nearby, guarding the door.

"Sure. Let's check out the landscape."

They were seated in the lower bar area of the long, luxurious Pullman lounge car. *Pleasure Dome* was the trademarked name for the viewing deck above. The lush seats, glare-proof glass, and Leo's pornographic conversation were bound to put Vivian into a stupor once they got up there. She rose to her feet, swaying against the rolling train. She'd consumed two glasses of wine.

"That was a joke. I ain't climbing up there."

"I wouldn't want you to have a heart attack, you fat ape."

Vivian grabbed her purse and walked past the tight little bar built into the lounge. The Negro bartender was an alert young man. He asked if she'd like another glass of burgundy. Or maybe some lunch? His tone implied she should lay a base of food under the wine. He offered to order a sandwich from the dining car and have it delivered to the lounge. She shook her head at the idea, nodded her chin at her wine glass, and leaned against the bar as he filled it up. He was a good-looking kid and held up his end of the conversation. Her attention to the boy was guaranteed to piss off Nutcracker Leo. She left a quarter on the bar and stumbled up to the private dining room. From there it was another short flight up to the Pleasure Dome.

It was empty, and she felt like a bird surrounded by all that sky. The landscape baked in the sun, whistling past at speed, and slowing down as her eyes focused on the flat horizon. She'd never seen the Great Plains, the wide expanse of tall grasses, accented by occasional clusters of colorful wildflowers. Seen from the train, it was dreamy and soft, with a shimmering of heat like a mirage. A beauty unspoiled by human hands, or so it seemed. Vivian knew from experience that pastoral paradises were an illusion. People worked this land. Farmers toiled from sunrise to sunset, struggling for survival. It was a world she had run away from. She'd rather remain on the train and enjoy it from afar.

She put on her sunglasses and settled into a soft chair. By habit, always aware of her surroundings, she positioned herself next to the railing, with a view of the people below. They'd arrive in Kansas City at one o'clock. She glanced at her wristwatch. Two more hours. The time alone felt good. Vivian had a lot to think about and couldn't do it with Abati and his two hairy thugs in close proximity. Her eyes drifted to the horizon again.

When they reached Kansas City, she had to call her contact and make sure Truman's agenda hadn't changed. They'd settled for a visit the President planned to make to the Kansas City Board of Trade on Tuesday afternoon, his last engagement before flying back to Washington. The building was downtown, surrounded by offices and apartments. The Reds had found a flat that offered a good view of the entrance Truman was expected to use. Vivian would have a narrow window to take a shot and no room for error. Crowds would clog the street, waiting for the official motorcade, and she could use the masses to cover her escape, when panic set in. None of that was easy but she would be in control, at liberty to decide up to the final moment whether to proceed or abort.

What she didn't control was the Abati situation. From the moment she had set foot on the platform in San Francisco, she had been tightly monitored. It was a miracle she managed to call Maggie. Once the Mob convention was underway, she hoped to have some freedom of movement. The men would be busy and Abati said there were other women along for the ride. They couldn't be kept locked up.

The Elms in Excelsior Springs. How far was it from KC? Transportation might be tricky.

And there was Tom Keegan to think about. His job was

to keep an eye on her, for protection. She chuckled. He hadn't been too good at that lately. Although she spotted a couple of guys who looked like cops, both on the Lark and on this train. It made sense that with Tom thrown off course by the Oakland diversion, some kind of cover had been put in place.

She'd have to give Tom and Abati the slip. Many eyes would be on her, too many maybe. The Truman job was going to be a challenge. That never stopped her before.

A man entered the lounge car below. Tall. Thin. Like a pencil. He had a long nose, weak chin, wore a gray hat. If her life were a movie, he'd play an accountant or scientist. Something was familiar about him, and she mulled it over as he folded himself in half and sat down. He waved at the kid behind the bar. The young man scampered over and took his order.

The sun felt warm on Vivian's face through the thick glass. She'd changed into her favorite red suit and looked more like a businesswoman than a whore. She *was* a businesswoman. *And* a whore. She rolled her head around on the leather seat back, imagining herself on a trip somewhere that didn't involve so much mattress action. The only real vacation trip she'd ever taken was to Havana three years before. It had been cut short by a crime boss who'd sent a woman to kill her. Kitty Hawk was her working name. All the big hitters had names like that. Gunselle, her own moniker, was at the end of its starring run. Vivian didn't mind. She had a lot of life left to live.

She stared at the pencil-thin man in the lounge. Something prickled under her skin. He definitely looked familiar. Then it came to her. The Eraser. What was he doing on the train? People like him, like her—contract killers—didn't travel for pleasure. Was he after Abati? Was he after her?

There was no escape on a high-speed train in open country. It was a tricky place to rub someone out, and, besides, how could the Eraser have predicted the switcheroo in San Francisco? It had to be a coincidence.

He couldn't possibly know her by sight, but she knew

him. She'd been hired to kill him way back in 1947, after he'd pumped slugs into Bugsy Siegel with an M1 rifle. The envelope she received came with photos. It was him. Donato Gomma, aka the Eraser. He fled to Italy before she could complete the job. She wondered if the contract was still open.

Gomma was sipping his beer, relaxed.

The country's top Mob operators were meeting in Kansas City and she'd been hired to shoot the President. And now another assassin was on his way to the same place. Vivian doubted the Eraser's ticket went all the way to Chicago.

Who was his target? Her first instinct said Abati, but it could be any other high-ranking mobster. Or maybe he was insurance if she couldn't deliver Truman … unless he was there to clean up after her, like she was hired to clean up after the Siegel hit. She felt a shiver. Gomma's presence complicated things even more. If Kansas City was indeed his final destination.

Mike Abati lowered himself gingerly into the chair beside her, oofing with pain. Vivian was so focused on Gomma, she hadn't seen him walk in. Aldo took a seat on Abati's other side, holding a bottle of beer in each hand.

"Everything work itself out?" She winked at Aldo.

"Finally," Abati said. "Damn hemorrhoids. My ass is killing me."

"How do you think I like it?"

He looked at her sideways. "Fair enough. Pussy from now on."

"Thanks. You're a gentleman, Mike."

The Eraser stared up at them with a sly grin on his face. He'd made Abati. Vivian hoped nothing would come of it.

Abati rambled on for the next hour about his wife and kids, caressing her knee between swigs of beer that Aldo ran up and down the stairs to fetch.

The train rolled into Union Station in Kansas City right on time.

*

Tom left his suitcase at the hotel and went to Union Station well ahead of the *Super Chief*'s arrival. Talking to Rachel had lifted a weight off his shoulders. He was rested and ready to tackle whatever Abati and his gorillas threw his way. He doubted they would cause trouble. They wouldn't risk attracting attention.

He bought a newspaper and tried to read, with one eye on the big station clock.

Kansas City was gearing up for a week of corporate events. The FFA, Future Farmers of America, was having its annual convention in the city, Avon as well, and the area's hotels and motor courts were filled to bursting. Tom had been lucky to find a room last night. The Chamber of Commerce was gushing about the events and the standing ovation President Truman, a native Missourian, was expected to receive. The article gave Tom a better appreciation of the problems Special Agent Thorpe and his troops were facing.

A garbled voice on the public address system announced the arrival of the *Super Chief*.

Tom made his way through the foot traffic to the platform. He planned to intercept Vivian before she entered the station proper. He kept the newspaper. He wasn't the only one waiting for train passengers. He stood next to a mother with two young children. At a glance, he would appear to be part of the family.

The big train came in slowly, with a shuffle of vapor and restrained power. It was easy to relive a childhood fascination with the big engines. There was something benevolent in that sleek metal giant that awakened the kid in Tom. That and the romantic notion of eating miles of country, under sun or starry sky. From the sea, through mountains, deserts, and endless prairie, to discover a new city with the promise of new beginnings. How many of those arriving today had left something behind they'd rather forget?

When passengers emerged, the level of activity picked up. Porters rushed along the platform, expectant family members waved and called, part excitement, part confusion.

Tom squinted. His height helped. He could see above the bobbing heads.

Mike Abati and his dark-suited bodyguards formed a tight black knot on the platform. Vivian wore a red suit that caught the light like a drop of fresh blood in the middle of an ink stain.

Tom watched the group come toward him. The muscle men each carried two suitcases. Their eyes scanned the platform, hard, aware, hyenas on the lookout for carrion. Tom studiously set his sight behind them and plastered a smile on his face. He waved at nobody in particular with the rolled newspaper.

The shadow of a smile and eye contact confirmed Vivian had spotted him. He made a chopping sign with a quick head move toward the exit. *Abort mission. Get out.* Her eyes went wide.

Then the expression on her face changed, turned tense. She shook her head and lifted her chin to motion at something behind Tom. He turned to see what caught her eye. He didn't notice anything out of the ordinary. People hurrying to the exit. Women dragging crying children by the arm. Men in suits and hats. FBI agents among them, no doubt.

They were close now, and Vivian mouthed *No.*

A couple seconds and it was too late to change the course of events, she was past him, surrounded by Abati and his men.

Tom pushed the bodies that were in his way. He caught a glimpse of the group near one of the exits. By the time he reached the doors through the mass of people, they were gone.

*

Special Agent Thorpe looked more disheveled than the day before. Colored pins dotted the big map now, and more pictures were displayed on the board.

"You brought the girl here?" Thorpe said when he saw Tom.

"No."

"They got rid of her?"

Tom lit a cigarette and sat on the corner of Thorpe's desk. "I signaled her to get out of there. It would have been easy. With the crowd, there's nothing Abati and his men could have done to stop her."

Thorpe leaned toward him. "And?"

"She saw something, I have no idea what, but it changed her mind. She left with Abati."

The agent shrugged. "He turned her."

Of course, Thorpe would jump to that conclusion. The woman was mercenary. She would go where the money was and the Mob was flush with it.

"You're not listening, Thorpe. She was coming to me and something made her change her mind. It must be damn important. She's no flake. I trust her."

"So what? Your girl had a change of mind. It's all hands on deck, Keegan. You think I care about the mood swings of a hooker?"

"She'll be at The Elms. I'm not asking for much. I'm her handler. Put me under cover at the hotel. What have you got to lose?"

Thorpe had to consider the offer. Why wouldn't he? Tom was one more officer on site to supplement his agents.

"Okay, but you better not get in the way." He motioned to a young man who'd just hung up a phone and was picking up another ringing one. "Gordon, this is Tom Keegan, SFPD, take care of him."

Tom's hackles went up at being shoved aside, but before he could protest Thorpe had walked away. He dropped the butt of his cigarette in a coffee cup, Thorpe's he hoped.

Gordon led him to a corner of the room, away from the ringing phones.

"You put the woman on the train with Abati."

It was a pleasant surprise to find somebody who was up to speed.

"I went to Union Station to pull her out and she refused. Something's going on. I need to get into The Elms."

Gordon sized him up, one eyebrow raised. "You'll never pass for hotel personnel. We have agents among the staff anyway, no need to duplicate efforts."

"I can't register as a guest," Tom said. "A single man at a resort sticks out like Santa on Easter Sunday." He had a thought for Rachel. If she was with him, things would be a lot easier.

Gordon considered the Kansas City map. "The Avon convention is in full swing at the hotel. It's an option but you'll be noticed, it's a bunch of ladies. We gave up on the idea because none of our guys looked the part. They're either kids fresh out of college or they reek of cop."

"A couple of female agents would be useful."

Gordon laughed. "Yeah. Imagine that ... broads ... Lots of trouble. Lots to worry about. Look at you, you're concerned about your girl and she's a seasoned pro."

Pro. Seasoned. "You have no idea," Tom muttered around the fresh cigarette he was lighting. "There are no men at that Avon meeting?"

"A few management types, a couple guest speakers ... but yeah, males are rare."

Tom took a long drag of his smoke. "I might be able to bluff my way in, but if they check my identity I'll be kicked out. Can you rig a cover?"

Gordon rummaged among piles of documents. "I have an Avon phone list somewhere. We gathered all we could find about the place and who would be there when we learned about The Elms. What bogus credentials are you thinking of?"

"Not a guest speaker, my area of expertise won't cut it. Something so boring nobody will want to know more about it." Avon made cosmetics and sold the stuff door to door. That was all he knew. "What about production planning?"

Gordon chuckled. "Big yawn. Assistant Manager or something similarly vague?"

"Perfect." Tom's experience with FBI agents was neutral at best, but he liked Gordon. Maybe the young man was too new in the job to have turned into a hardass like

Thorpe or a pompous prick like Burdon.

Gordon held a typed page. "They have a big plant in Morton Grove, Illinois, north of Chicago. Ever been?"

"Don't know Morton Grove, but Chicago, yeah, couple of times."

"Let's give them a call. It's better if you go under your real name, in case somebody wants to see a driver's license."

"My California license."

"You're a recent transfer. No big deal. What's your full name?"

"Thomas Glen Keegan. Glen with one N."

Ten minutes later Mike Ogilvy, the Morton Grove plant manager, had a new employee. Without missing a beat Gordon asked one of the phone operators to reserve a room for Tom at The Elms.

"Tell them he's with the Avon group," he said. "They have a block reservation."

Tom had to admit the guy was efficient.

"There are strings attached, Keegan."

To be expected. "Like what?"

"You call me if you learn anything fishy. About Truman or something else." Gordon scribbled a phone number on a card. "Talk to Thorpe if I'm unavailable, but not Burdon, or your pals in San Francisco. We run this as a separate setup. Got it?"

"Meaning that if it goes haywire at The Elms, I'm on my own."

Gordon nodded.

"Where is that hotel?"

Gordon showed him on the map. Excelsior Springs. Thirty miles northeast of town. Far enough to be inconvenient if Tom had to make a quick getaway with Vivian. He needed a car. It was unlikely Gordon would lend him one. This gig was off the books.

Tom pointed at the bleak photos pinned on the board. "I recognize Abati, who are the others?"

"They're not all big names, but they all have long

sheets. Top row, left to right. Sam 'Momo' Giancana. Heard of him?" Tom nodded. "Lotteries, gambling, liquor, he's got his claws into Louisiana and his eyes on Chicago. On his way to the summit of the mountain. Ambitious. Brains. Not going to let anybody stand in his way. He's the high-profile character on site. Next to him, his buddy, Santo 'Sonny' Trafficante. He looks like an insurance salesman, but don't be fooled. Florida and Cuba are his. Oodles of money. Together these two call the shots. They're not in town yet. Won't be long before they roll in."

"Serious business won't start without them," Tom said.

"Correct. On the next level you have the brothers Giacalone, Anthony and Vito, from Denver. Friends of Sam. Then Joey Piranio, from Dallas. Your man, Abati, is on that level, with the local KC heavy, Anthony Gizzo, who's hosting the event. The rest are smaller fry and foot soldiers. All armed to the teeth."

Tom pulled out his smokes, offered the pack to Gordon who checked over his shoulder before taking one. He held the stick in his cupped hand and leaned over to take a puff. Like a kid afraid to get knuckle-rapped. It made Tom smile.

"Any idea if there are opposing factions in the group?"

"Not publicly acknowledged, but these guys have sharp teeth. The business is cutthroat."

"You must have an inkling of why they're meeting."

"Your guess is as good as mine," Gordon said. "Money and territory are always popular topics. They're all on the rise, relatively young, which means tensions and jostling for position. No love lost between them. Giancana and Trafficante want to remain on top and can't tolerate small dogs nipping at their heels. Part of the meeting must be about building alliances, fostering loyalty. And the opposite, getting a fix on potential adversaries. Then there's the dope market, the new money machine. Who gets what from that fat sow."

"Looks like everything's on the table. It'll keep them busy. Your outfit denies organized crime exists, but you're well-informed."

Gordon took one long drag and crushed the cigarette under a shoe heel, careful to swipe the evidence under a desk. "I'm based in Chicago. I know how it rolls. Hoover has blinders but the guys in the field have eyes to see. The Director is focused on the President. There have been multiple threats. Serious intel. It's no joke, Keegan. That's why we're here in force. I pushed to use the proximity with the Mob. The more we know about these guys the better."

It explained why Gordon was on the ball with the Abati scheme.

"So, the moment Truman leaves, safe and sound, you pack up your pins, your boards, and your phones?"

Gordon shrugged. "And we'll consider ourselves lucky. After seventy-two hours of total madness."

Tom didn't want to think how much this troop movement would cost the taxpayer. As long as the Prez got out alive. His main takeaway from the conversation was that as soon as Truman hightailed it out of town, Vivian and he would be left hanging with nobody giving a rat's ass what happened to them.

11. Sunday, May 4

Vivian looked for Tom Keegan's tall frame in the crowd as the cab pulled out of Union Station. Did her attempt to point out Gomma on the platform get through to him? Abati and the boys had crushed in around her. She peered over their shoulders.

"You lose something?" said Leo from the front seat, next to the cabbie.

"No, but you did."

"What did I lose?"

"Your brain. I saw it fall out on the sidewalk when you hailed the cab. A kid picked it up. He must have thought it was a walnut."

The cabbie chuckled.

The ride to Excelsior Springs took half an hour. It was hot as hell in the cab because it was hot as hell in Missouri. And it was only May. Vivian dripped in her tight outfit. She could smell the ripe odor coming off her.

"I need a shower as soon as we get to the hotel."

"You'll have to make it quick, Queenie. We're heading out to join the other parties at the opening of the cattle show as soon as we drop off our bags. We're getting in a day late. We're short on time."

"I'll be quick, but I need to change into something cooler. Jesus Christ, I'm melting."

"I'll keep the cab running. 'Four-eyes' doesn't hit the podium until five o'clock."

"Four-eyes?"

"Truman. He's the main speaker."

Vivian remembered that piece of information from her briefing with the Reds. The President opened the show. She began to sweat even more. Could the Eraser go for the hit straight off the train? Brazen. Effective too. She shivered in her hot suit. What to do? Let it slide and keep her mouth shut? If Truman was the Eraser's objective, what was it to her? She wouldn't have to return the down payment. And she could score points with Tom Keegan. Give him the Eraser. The pencil-man was competition and a threat somewhere down the line. Vivian rubbed her back against the seat. The suit itched in all the wrong places. Where was Tom when she needed him? She looked through the cab's rear window. There was a car behind them, at a distance. It could be him.

"Hey Queenie, lighten up." Abati poked her in the ribs. "We're almost there."

Farmland separated Kansas City and Excelsior Springs as they drove north on Highway 69. The ride seemed to take forever. Vivian's armpits drained sweat into her suit. She wasn't the only one who reeked, and it all seemed so unimportant right now.

They turned at an intersection and there was no car behind them anymore.

She had to find a phone and call Maggie to get a message to Pete Delgado.

Vivian couldn't kick loose from the men in the hotel lobby. She took the key from Leo at the reception desk and ran upstairs with her suitcase. Aldo was right behind her, stickier than glue.

She unlocked the door and rushed to the bathroom. She stripped and showered, dried herself quickly. She'd brought one summer dress, a flower-patterned off-the shoulder number. She slipped into it. It was instantly refreshing.

The men had no interest in cleaning up. Abati yelled at her to get her ass out of the bathroom and hurry downstairs, she was putting them behind.

After a look in the mirror, Vivian grabbed her purse and navigated her way past the myriad banquet rooms, meeting rooms, and ballrooms in the sprawling hotel. Aldo was close on her heels, as persistent and keen-eyed as a herding sheepdog. Signs pointed to the spa and alleged healing waters. She noticed groups of women in the lobby. Another conference? Daughters of the American Revolution? What a combustible combination, proper housewives and musclebound goons.

Leo and Abati stood next to the cab, smoking. The cabbie might be able to retire on the proceeds of this one fare.

"Finally," said Abati. "Get in. You look like a wet dream, but we're behind schedule."

"Art takes time." Vivian slid into the back seat and gave Aldo's knee a squeeze as he got in on her left. He kept her from a phone, but his big dog loyalty was endearing. Abati flopped in on her right and shouted at the cabbie.

"American Royal Cattle Show. And step on it."

Vivian sweltered all over again on the ride back to the city. She would have to drink some water soon or she'd pass out from dehydration. Every time she closed her eyes, she had visions of Tom Keegan's gray fedora. No way he could keep up with her hectic moves of the past hour.

The windows were down on each side of the car and the breeze helped, but she was crushed between two hulking men.

The smell of the stockyards hit them a few blocks from their destination. Vivian had grown up on a farm with a couple of dairy cows in the barn. She'd milked them, patted their flanks, and shoveled their shit. Men weren't much different. The stench of the hairy animals was sometimes overpowering, but she could take it. Same with the cows.

"Jesus, boss," Leo said, as the car crested a ramp that brought them to the entrance of the stockyards building. He held a hanky over his nose. There were tears in his hooded eyes.

"Welcome to the West Bottoms," said the driver. "I'm sure you heard about the big flood last year. Nearly destroyed everything. Stockyards. Packing plants. But the cattle, as you can tell, are back."

They climbed out. Leo paid the man and Vivian surveyed the sun-drenched scene. The river glimmered in the background, half a mile away. A checkerboard of pens spread out as far as the eye could see, a reeking quilt separated by pathways and ramps for directing four-legged traffic to the slaughterhouse. Rows of train tracks, ten lanes wide ran up to the pens on all sides. Not a pay phone in sight. What use would they be to a cow about to be butchered?

The sounds of a brass band tooted from inside the massive hall. They went in and Vivian had a full view of the arena. A ring of high overhead windows let the thick air crawl out. The smell wasn't too bad, thanks to the enticing odor of barbecue.

Abati and the boys aimed for a cluster of men in dark suits and fedoras. When Abati was recognized, backslapping began. Vivian stood behind her boss and made eye contact with a well-built redhead in the other group.

"Queenie, meet Joey Piranio. He runs things in Dallas. Haven't seen him in years."

"Queenie. Yeah, I can see how you got your name. Maybe you want to dump this chump and come settle in with Muriel and me."

Abati winked and poked her in the ribs. Piranio motioned for the redhead to move into the circle. She shook hands with Vivian and stepped back into the shadows.

"Maybe Muriel and I could have coffee in the morning," Vivian said. "Soak in the pool together. I wouldn't mind making a friend while I'm here."

"What about me and the boys?" Abati said, quick to take umbrage.

Vivian grinned, showing a lot of teeth.

"Sure," Piranio said. "Have a cup with my girl. I can't keep her occupied every hour of the day. I'm seventy-four."

The men laughed.

"You do all right." Muriel's eyes found Vivian's. She was visibly tense.

The group moved to the concession area and perused the spice-rubbed meat sizzling on the open grills. The air wasn't getting any cooler around the glowing charcoal.

Vivian ordered a pulled-pork sandwich. She asked the clerk for French fries and a root beer and carried everything to a picnic table where she settled down to eat.

"What the fuck are you doing, Queenie?" Abati

growled. "We got people to meet."

"I'm hungry. I'll catch up."

"Aldo. Stay with her. We'll be in front near the podium. Bring her down as soon as she's done stuffing herself." Abati turned to Piranio. "If she wasn't such a hot number in the sack, I'd fucking mash her face the way she drives me nuts."

"Mike." Vivian raised a finger to her lips. "There are families present."

The woman across from her wore a red-trimmed hat, and a face just as red as she held her hands over her small boy's ears. The man next to her had gotten to his feet, fists clenched, unsure how much of a scene to make in front of all the tough guys. Vivian motioned downward with her flat hand, and the man took his seat again.

Abati and Piranio, Muriel and the goons following, walked to the stairs and disappeared down toward the open floor of the arena.

"I'm gonna grab some grub, too." Aldo rubbed his hands together.

"Take your time." Vivian smiled at the woman in the red hat. "Don't mind my boss. His manners could curdle cottage cheese. That's a cute kid."

The woman's husband thought Vivian was cute too. His eyeballs gave him away.

Aldo returned quickly—too quickly for Vivian to plan anything—with a plate of ribs and a stack of paper napkins. The couple dumped their waste into a large metal drum and moved off with their kid.

If only Tom Keegan would appear with some brisket and coleslaw. She'd ask Aldo to get her another root beer. Then she'd have a couple of minutes with her favorite detective. Only he was nowhere to be seen, and Truman was about to deliver his speech. She scanned the rafters looking for the spot she would have chosen to take the shot. The shadows were thick. A good set-up. She shrugged. Nothing she could do. She chatted with Aldo over French fries. He enjoyed pretending to be her boyfriend. More squares sat down at the table with their lunch and innocence. Then a booming voice came over the loudspeakers. It was time.

"Crap," Aldo said. "We need to get down there."

"Bullshit, lover boy. You'd rather sit up here and stare at my tits."

"Ma'am!" said a woman seated at the table across from Vivian with her twin girls. The little blondes lapped at ice cream cones.

"Sorry kids." Vivian hauled Aldo up by the arm. "Let's get down there, Junior. And wipe the sauce off your face." She seemed to have to tell him to clean himself up all the time. Lipstick, barbecue sauce. It was a miracle the boy was potty-trained.

12. Sunday, May 4

Tom recovered his suitcase from the hotel. It felt heavier than the day before. The temperature was climbing. Kansas City was nothing like San Francisco in the spring.

Union Station had a car rental office. Unfortunately, with all the visitors' activity in town, they didn't have a single vehicle left in the lot.

"You should have made a reservation, sir," the employee scolded.

Tom resisted barking back. It wouldn't help one bit. "Is there a garage nearby, a place where I could get a loaner?"

The employee made a face. Garages were competition.

"You don't have a car available for rent, sport," Tom said. "It isn't like you're sending business away."

After a brief huffing bout, the man pointed him to the Williams Garage a few blocks away. Off Tom went, lugging his suitcase. The temperature had gone up several degrees more and he could feel his shirt sticking to his back. By now the shoulder holster with the heavy Colt sat in a puddle.

The garage was a two-story building at the end of a brick block, four bays with an office facing the street, and a drive-thru to a lot behind where a few cars baked in the sun. A bald man in his fifties, wearing blue overalls, sat in the office behind a metal desk that might have come from Army surplus.

"Mr. Williams?" Tom pulled out his badge. "I'm a detective from San Francisco, in town following a case. I'm looking for a car I could borrow." He anticipated what came next and explained. "They have no rentals available at the train station."

The man stared at the badge. "Far away from home."

"I'll put a fifty on it." It was generous, and the glimmer in Williams's eyes was promising. "I'll need the car for a week."

"We're not in the rental business." Williams shook his head. "What's wrong with cabs?"

"If I'm trying to catch a thief, Mr. Williams, calling a

cab isn't convenient." Tom pulled out his wallet. He riffled through the banknotes.

"Can I see that?" Williams pointed a knobby finger at the picture Tom had pushed aside to get to the bills.

It was a small photograph, ragged on the edges from having been shuffled around. Tom hesitated. The picture was a treasured memory. Williams's smile convinced him to hand it over.

"Where was this taken?" Williams said.

"Bavaria. At the end."

"Good friends still?"

Tom nodded. "Pete Barnaby, from Missouri actually, near Saint Louis. I'm still driving the old beater Ford his cousin sold me. Wish I had it right now."

Williams gave him the picture back. He reached in a desk drawer, and pulled out a photograph, larger than the one Tom carried in his wallet. Kids—they always all looked like kids—posed next to a tank. "My son was over there. Third Army, with Patton."

"They got us out of trouble in Bastogne." Tom was careful to keep his tone neutral. Did Williams lose a son in the war?

"Ben was injured in Metz, busted knee." Williams pondered. "Maybe we can work something out." His expression turned sly. "If you do something for me."

Tom waited.

"You were a captain over there. You saw things you probably don't care to recall. Talk to Ben. I think it would do him good."

"It's a strange thing to ask for, Mr. Williams. You don't know me."

"You lived through it, like Ben. He was a unit mechanic. His knee was crushed in an accident, pulling the engine out of a Sherman tank. Hurts him bad, and he takes dope for the pain, but he won't talk about it. Won't do anything but work all the time. He never goes out, never sees friends for a beer. He's a good kid, but he's wound tight.

Maybe he'll let loose with you and get that sludge out of his head. Then I'll rent you a car." He pointed behind him. "It's in the lot, a Dodge Coronet, six-cylinder, goes up to 90. You can catch thieves with that, Mr. Keegan."

Tom sighed. He never talked about the war years. There was nothing to say, meaning there was too much to say. That time in his life was as remote as the Moon.

"You're offering a trade."

"My boy's in the workshop."

The shop was as neat as the office. Clanging sounds came from under a green Oldsmobile. The banging competed, out of sync, with the swinging strains of Anita O'Day and Gene Krupa coming from a radio on the workbench.

"Ben Williams?" Tom said.

A young man, gaunt face and blond spiky hair, rolled out from underneath the car. He sat up and wiped his hands on a rag. His overalls were the duplicate of his father's, but grimier. He was good-looking, with cloudy blue eyes. He leaned to the left and winced when he got to his feet, favoring a bad leg.

"Can I help you?"

"Your father and I made a deal. A car on loan in exchange for a conversation."

"Can't be much of a car, unless it's a damn good conversation."

Tom held out his hand. "Tom Keegan."

They shook. Ben's grip was firm, a little too much so.

"Gotta be honest," Tom said. "It isn't just the words. I'll also be fifty dollars leaner."

"That's more like Pop." Ben squinted. "You served?"

"It's that obvious?"

"Takes one to know one." He turned off the radio. "Who were you with?"

"One hundred and first."

Ben shook his head. "Wouldn't get me up there. What's it like to jump into a hole?"

Tom grinned. "The air doesn't hurt. It's the ground

you have to watch out for."

Ben chuckled. He motioned at the back door. "There's a place to sit over there, in the shade."

Tom pulled out his pack of cigarettes and offered it to Ben. He noticed the needle tracks on the young man's forearms.

They went outside. The blue Dodge shimmered, a mirage under the sun.

"That's a sweet ride." Tom pulled out his lighter. He lit Ben's cigarette before his own.

"The Williams Garage's pride. It's hard on my knee."

"Still hurts, eh?"

"You have sharp eyes, Keegan. It took you one glance to know I was on the juice."

"My eyesight isn't good enough to get the specifics. What are you taking?"

"Morphine." Ben shrugged. "Our family doc is a veteran. Free car repairs. I'm careful. Pop doesn't need to worry about it. It's only when the pain drives me nuts."

Tom wanted to believe the man. He didn't look like a doper. The back-breaking physical labor of an auto mechanic was an unlikely tonic for a bum leg. "Your father thinks I can help. I've no idea how."

"Pop has notions. He went over in the first one. Belleau Wood. Mud-filled trenches. Gas. Talk about a shit show." Ben tapped his cigarette against his injured knee. "Makes me feel like a faker. I spun a wrench all day behind the lines. Never fired a rifle."

Tom leaned forward, his hands between his knees, studying the dust in the courtyard. "We were damn lucky we didn't end in a box. We answered a call and went. After that, people made decisions for us, some good, some rotten, and we came back changed. And there's things that stick in our heads. You and I, your Pop, we got our lives back. What happens next is on us." He shrugged off the objection he could see coming. "Yeah, it isn't completely in our control. The *Welcome Home* banners are gone. So what? We went to hell and back. Some journey."

"I was a mechanic in a garage when I left, worked on tanks, and I'm still a mechanic. Just more banged up. Yeah, some journey." Ben took nervous puffs from the cigarette. "I live over the garage in a two-bedroom apartment. I try not to think about how nice it would be if I could meet a girl and settle down with her up there. Put that second bedroom to use. Ma would sure like a grandkid to coo over."

"I don't blame her. Where do boys go to meet girls these days?"

"Regular girls like to dance. My rhythm is off."

"Not all girls measure a man by his dancing skills. A smart one will come your way." Tom pointed at the Dodge, glistening like a wet mermaid. "I bet you tuned the heck out of that engine. How fast can it go?"

Ben Williams pulled himself together. "I pushed it to 120. If Pop knew, he'd blow a gasket." He shrugged. "Okay, you talk a good game. I bet you were an officer."

"Major bullshitter, you mean. I had plans before the war. I wanted to be a lawyer, with a nice office and a club membership. After the shit show, as you called it, that life didn't cut it anymore."

Ben took a long look at the wrinkled traveling salesman suit. "So now you roam the country in rental cars, talking to winged vets on the side?"

"I'm a murder cop in San Francisco. My job keeps me on my toes. It's immediate. Not much time to let the mind wander. I like that." He smiled. "I try to fix things. I bet you're better at it than I am."

Ben pushed himself off the bench. "Neither of us will ever be out of a job. I'll get the car keys."

*

"We're almost fully booked, Mr. Keegan," the hotel receptionist said. "I can't put you in the east wing with the other Avon delegates. You'll be in the west wing, room four twenty-six. I hope it isn't too much of an inconvenience."

"Not at all. I'm sorry the call came in so late. Some

confusion at the office." He looked at the lobby. "I thought I would have to camp outside."

"We have another gathering in the west wing. You know the Rodeo is about to start? It's more than bull riding, broncos, and the like. A lot of business is conducted during the festivities. From what I understand, the gentlemen meeting here are in the meat processing industry."

Meat processing, somebody in the goon squad had a sense of humor.

The receptionist handed Tom his chunky room key. He pointed. "The main conference room is over there. That's where the Avon ladies have their registration counter."

"Can I get my suit pressed?" Tom said.

"Of course, sir. Just call the main number when you're ready and somebody will come and pick it up."

It always amazed Tom how much information a simple polite conversation could deliver. The mobsters gathered in the hotel's west wing, where they also had their rooms, and by a stroke of luck he was lodged in the same area. He should collect his Avon badge to avoid raising suspicion.

He changed into his gray suit and called reception to have the blue one taken care of and his shirts laundered. Then he walked the length of the fourth floor to reach the safety of the east wing where the Avon meeting was taking place. He was intrigued. He had never attended a conference where women were the overwhelming majority. Was it different than other sales conventions? Less drinking and better behavior, hopefully.

The lady sitting behind the registration desk was middle-aged and pleasant. Surprised by his arrival, but he knew the right names. Morton Grove. Mike Ogilvy.

"Have you attended one of our meetings before, Mr. Keegan?" she asked.

"It's my first. They don't let us production people out much."

She laughed. "And what a shame that is. Without you we wouldn't have anything to sell."

"That swings both ways. Without you, my machines wouldn't have anything to do."

She gave him a sheet with the schedule of speakers and group presentations.

"Proceedings are over for the day, but most delegates are still in the conference room, enjoying cocktails. There's a gala dinner on the last day, after our regional manager's closing remarks. People gather informally for lunch and dinner. We have reserved tables in the main restaurant." She leaned closer to him. "That is the best part, Mr. Keegan, the get-togethers. Meeting people, making friends." She smiled. "You should have no problems making friends."

He was aware of her eyes sliding to his hands. No wedding band. He pinned the badge to his lapel. He was official.

The ballroom was colorful. Put a hundred men in dark suits together in a room and you have a wake. Assemble a hundred women and it's a completely different atmosphere. Even if many of them wore suits. Tom spotted a handful of male attendees, like dark ferns in a fragrant bouquet. Nicely fragrant thanks to the perfume and cosmetics samples displayed on tables along the walls. A banner proclaiming *Welcome 1952 Avon Stars* hung above the speaker's platform. Attendees were clustered between the round tables with their circle of chairs. A squad of servers worked the room with glasses on trays. Conversations and laughter were similarly bubbly.

Tom aimed for the displays. Might as well learn something about the company he was supposed to work for.

He was reading about the fastest lipstick assembly line in the world—250 lipsticks per minute, 300,000 lipsticks a day—trying to picture what the pile would look like in the conference room when he felt a tap on his shoulder.

The woman smiled and it lit up her entire face. Tom smiled in response. She reminded him of one of the efficient nurses who worked dreary shifts in field hospitals, never ruffled, not when a wounded soldier was in range anyway.

She held out her hand. "June Cavendish, nice to meet you."

They shook hands. Tom pointed at his badge. "Tom Keegan."

"Are you into lipstick, Tom?"

He laughed. "*Double Dare Red*. Who can resist?"

"Can I quote you? I'm in advertising." She reached for a passing champagne tray and took two glasses. "What are you doing for this wonderful company?"

"Production planning."

She nodded. "It's a complicated process, isn't it?"

"What are you working on, June? Any exciting campaigns in the making?"

"You missed my presentation?"

"I'm afraid I did. I just got in."

She took his arm and led him around the room. "Let me show you."

For the next twenty minutes, Tom was treated to an overview of the advertisements that would grace the pages of Rachel's magazines in the coming months. He planned to make good use of the inside information. The champagne was excellent. By the time they completed the circuit of posters and displays, they had both downed three glasses.

Tom was spared awkward parting words when a young woman came to tell June she had a phone call. He thanked her for the presentation and left the room as soon as she was out of sight.

It was still too early to hang around the watering holes that should attract the wildlife he was here to hunt. He went back to his room and ordered a sandwich from room service. Considering the quality of the champagne, he was sure the food would be an enormous improvement over the night before.

13. Sunday, May 4

A couple of folding chairs had been saved in the second row, directly in front of the podium. Vivian and Aldo squeezed in to take their seats under Abati's searing glare. She expected a vigorous spanking later that night.

Truman walked on stage all rumpled in a tan suit that made him look as compact as a brick. The heat had taken its toll on him too and he'd loosened his tie. His round spectacles were greeted with a smattering of applause and more than a few raucous jeers. Secret Service agents stood rooted to the podium not far from him. Their stone faces hunted the hecklers, nodding toward agents wandering the floor, directing traffic, hoping to intercept trouble. Did they check the rafters? If the Eraser was up there, Vivian thought he had a fair chance of making a clean escape. And if he succeeded in taking out the President, she wondered how hard it might be to convince her Commie cohorts that she'd had a hand in it. The extra ten grand would go a long way toward helping her forget Abati. She looked around for cameras. In case one caught her not firing a shot. The venue was packed and the organizers had let in more people than the tight rows of chairs allowed. The jeers came from the back where it was standing room only. Press photographers had their hungry lenses trained on the hecklers.

Over and over during his speech, Truman proclaimed his confidence that America would win the Cold War. Vivian grew hotter and more uncomfortable as the president labored to sound upbeat. She felt a little sorry for the man and hoped his legacy wouldn't end here, between barbecue pits and cattle chutes. She tensed when he wrapped things up, waiting for the crack of the rifle, the screams of the crowd, and the rushing around of men in suits, but the President finished his long-winded speech with his head intact.

A booming loudspeaker ordered the seated crowd to its feet, and the chairs were cleared to make room for the assembly of a portable dance floor. The brass band skedaddled and boys in matching red cowboy outfits began setting up their country swing gear.

Abati and his buddies huddled together to puff on cigars. None of the molls seemed interested in talking to Vivian. They watched her. Their group included Muriel. Vivian was the outsider, the unknown quantity.

It was after seven p.m. when the bosses broke their chatting circle and Vivian hoped the men planned to get out of this furnace. Abati danced over to her with a ragged cigar clamped between his teeth.

"We're heading downtown, baby. Sinatra is warbling at the Drum Lounge tonight. A private show. You up for some air-conditioned fun?"

"You call the plays. I'll dig the ways." Maggie used hepcat lingo all the time and Vivian hated it. It was fun to annoy someone else for a change. She was ready to strut her stuff if the club was indeed cool enough and she didn't have to strip down to her underwear to dance. "Is the cab still outside?"

"You'll dig this. Trafficante rented a bus for the week. A specially outfitted Greyhound to haul us around. Plushy seats, a full bar, and a jazz combo. We'll save a fortune on cabs." He laughed. "Trafficante likes to organize things."

Vivian cupped her hands in front of her mouth and shouted at the assemblage of dark-suited gangsters. "All aboard the THUG WAGON!"

Someone laughed. It wasn't Abati. His scowl promised retribution. Vivian was beyond caring.

The ride downtown took ten minutes—just long enough for a round of drinks—and the comfortable bus deposited the crime conventioneers in front of the elegant lobby doors of the prestigious, fifteen-floor, President Hotel. One of the thugs pointed down the sidewalk to another entrance at the corner. The chill behind the green doors sucked them into the Drum Lounge, a large room decorated in a South Seas motif with a stage at one end. In the center was a circular bar manned by three bartenders in white coats. It was meant to look like a drum, with a chrome rim around the edge at drinking level.

Sinatra hadn't hit the stage yet. Mobsters gathered around the drum. The barkeeps would be kept busy. Vivian took Muriel by the arm before she could be claimed by her boss's entourage and led her to a small table near the stage. It sat four, and two molls were already planted there. Vivian snapped her fingers at Aldo. Time for the men to wait on them for a change. Aldo trotted over, eager.

"Ladies," said Vivian. "What are you drinking?"

The women placed their orders with Aldo. He hurried off, looking proud of himself.

"He's cute," said a petite blonde in a tight green dress, straight hair down her back. She reminded Vivian of Veronica Lake. "Like a puppy dog. You work for him?"

"Good Heavens, no. Just a dumb kid wrapped around my finger. He's okay."

"I'm Vicki," said the blonde. She was small-boned, pretty, and spare in the breast department. "I'm here with Kid Cann. Minneapolis."

"Are you a rental?"

She looked at the floor, her lips pursed. "His regular girl."

"I'm Queenie, out of San Francisco. Here with Mike Abati. We should wear name tags." She waited for Muriel to introduce herself. It didn't happen. "This is Muriel. She's with the Dallas boss."

"We know Muriel," Vicki said.

The other girl was a stunner. Mixed race and shapely in a purple dress. She wore a flat hat pinned to her hair. Her skin was buttery brown, her eyes dark, lashes long, her lips full and succulent. Vivian gave her the once over. With a smile.

"I'm Jasmine," said the woman.

"Who are you with?"

"You ask too many questions." Jasmine lit a cigarette.

"I have a curious mind."

"That's a good way to end up dead. In a gutter. Your curiosity dribbling out."

Aldo returned with a tray of drinks. Champagne for Vicki and Muriel. Straight whiskey for Jasmine. He handed Vivian a large glass of red wine. She winked at him.

"Anything else I can get you ladies?"

"You can get lost," Jasmine said.

Aldo backed away from the table in silence. Vivian felt bad for him. He didn't deserve the rebuke. She would spend some time with him tomorrow, exploring the hotel grounds.

"Have any of you girls heard Sinatra live before? Sounds like we're going to have an intimate show tonight."

"I heard him get off inside me about a year ago. That was intimate." Jasmine tapped her cigarette on the edge of a glass ashtray. "After a performance at Baker's. In Detroit. He's got quite a voice for a scrawny Italian punk."

"He fucked me, too," Vicki said. "He won't remember me."

Vivian waited for Muriel to speak. She nodded. "Golly. I feel left out. The downside of being a rental, I suppose."

"Where's that dumb blonde Abati usually brings to meetings?" Jasmine crossed one knee over the other.

"She broke an ankle, or a leg, or something."

"How inconvenient. Glad you could fill in on such short notice."

Vivian could feel the sting of Jasmine's distrust. "It's usually square married men for me but I get these girlfriend jobs sometimes. It's nice to leave town."

"You don't have to convince me you're not a cop."

The band set up and the girls fell silent. Vivian wanted to probe them some more but Jasmine's attitude made her wary. After a second glass of wine, the urge to pee crept up on her. She got to her feet, walked out of the Drum Lounge, and found herself alone in the hotel lobby. For the first time in days no one was watching her. Waves of clapping and cheers streamed out of the Lounge. Sinatra must have been introduced. Vivian saw her chance; the goon squad would be distracted. She spotted a telephone and raced over, feeling in her pockets for change. As she reached the door of the booth, someone grabbed her arm. Aldo had her in his grip.

"What are you doing, Queenie? You can't make a phone call out here."

"Why not? I just want to call my sister. I don't go out of town much. I don't want her to worry."

"It's dangerous. There's always danger around Mike. Cops wanting to catch him, and other things."

She rolled her eyes. "You don't think cops know we're here? We travel in a bus for God's sake."

"I have my orders," Aldo said. "I have to stay with you, to protect you."

"That's nice. Mike said something about phones?"

"No, but you should ask him."

She patted his shoulder. "All right, I will. I don't want to get you in trouble. Stand by the door, I need to use the restroom."

When she was finished in the bathroom, Aldo escorted her across the lobby. The hotel was quiet on a Sunday night, except for the jazzy action in the Lounge. A man stood at the front desk, his back to her. He was checking in.

It was Gomma. With a suitcase. He was staying there. Vivian watched him take the stairs rather than the elevator. His room must be on the second or third floor. Thinking Aldo had that big gun under his arm …

Sinatra was in full croon by the time she and Aldo entered the Lounge. Vivian danced once with Aldo, making him beam with pleasure, then a few times with various bosses and lieutenants. Sinatra seemed drunk. He leered at her all night, especially while singing "I've Got You Under My Skin." Her looks had caught his eye. He was still married to that glamorous hurricane of a movie star, but something told Vivian every woman he laid eyes on got under his skin. Frankie left her cold. He was all hard angles, his face gaunt, and he still looked like a kid. A kid with a bad habit. She wondered what her lookalike movie star saw in him besides money and notoriety.

She pretended it was Tom Keegan in her arms for the

next song. She studied the molls while she was shuffled around the dance floor. Muriel and Vicki gazed up at Frank while they danced. Jasmine sat at the table and smoldered. Staring at Vivian.

At the end of "Body and Soul" Vivian smiled at her partner, not remembering his name, and brushed his hand off her ass. She sat down at Abati's table and leaned back in her chair, perspiring after her exertions on the dance floor. She could hear the men talking at the table behind her.

"Rumor has it that little shit went to the feds. Told Hoover he'd squeal on Giancana. A hundred bucks says someone puts a bullet in his head tonight."

"You're on," said another thug.

Vivian nearly tipped over backwards in her chair. Gomma. Sinatra. Truman. Way too many targets. Somebody was bound to catch a bullet.

*

It was after eleven when Tom went in search of a double whiskey. The hotel main bar was strategically positioned between the two wings. On the way, he located a couple of restaurants and the spa, with a heated swimming pool, deserted at this time of night. It was a potential meeting place, especially with the back door giving access to the gardens and the outside pool. He peeked into the bar but didn't go inside, wanting to explore the property first, to gain a perspective of routes and obstacles.

The parking lot was fuller than when he drove in. Big black Buicks and Cadillacs, with the occasional Chevrolet thrown in. Mobster rides. It looked like the top guys had arrived.

The bar wasn't busy. Avon ladies didn't come down at night for a nip. Two muscular types in boxy suits leaned on one end of the counter, in deep conversation. Bodyguards for one of the bosses. They didn't look like the two that traveled with Abati. Tom grabbed a newspaper from the rack and ordered from the bartender. He took his drink to an armchair in the back with a good view of the two entrances, one from the restaurant, the other from the hallway.

The entire Sunday paper was about the rodeo. While Tom was haggling with the FBI and talking to Ben Williams about the horrors of war, a happy citizen had won the barbecue competition and Truman had delivered the opening speech. Some people were having a swell time. Music and dancing. Were Thorpe and Gordon catching a breath at the FBI command post? The President was alive and well, so far.

Tom wondered if the bodyguards at the bar wished they were downtown for the fun and games. The Elms resort was posh but remote. What was there to do here for a gunslinger?

A young man in a tweed jacket entered the bar. He took a quick look around, got a drink from the barkeep, and made a beeline to Tom's corner.

He pointed at the badge that made a white spot on Tom's breast pocket. "Looks like we belong to the same club."

"Oh. I forgot to take if off." Tom smiled.

"Mark Jorgenson, Sales."

"Tom Keegan, Production. Are you in charge of the ladies?"

Jorgenson chuckled. "And how. They're sweet but they drive me ragged."

Tom knocked his glass against Jorgenson's. "The backbone of our business."

"You're one of the presenters tomorrow?"

"Hell no. I would put everybody to sleep. Nobody wants to hear about clogged pumps and greasy screws; it kills the magic."

Jorgenson stretched in his chair. He sipped his drink. "Boy, am I glad to meet somebody I can have a glass with. I wandered in here yesterday and retreated super quick with my tail between my legs. See the cavemen at the counter?"

Tom put down his newspaper. Truman waved from the front page. "Hard to miss. The guy at reception told me there's a meeting going on in the west wing. Meat processing, cattle business. These guys look like they have the shoulders for it."

"There was a dozen of them here last night. Slabs of beef, an entire wall of them. They looked at me like I was a squashed bug on the linoleum." Jorgenson shook his head. "I'm not wearing my badge around here anymore."

Tom nodded at the entrance. "I'm sure their girls wouldn't mind samples."

Four satin-clad high-heeled women entered the bar. They were followed by a trio of gorillas in bulging black suits—bulging with muscles and metal. Tom scanned and discarded them. Vivian wasn't in the group. The two goons at the counter got busy with chairs and stools. They looked like birds in a hurry to build a nest. Tom repressed a smile and buried his nose in his glass.

"Okay. Call me a coward, but I'm out of here," Jorgenson said.

"You don't believe in peaceful coexistence, Mark?"

"I'm not sure *they* do. See you tomorrow." He winked. "Maybe."

Tom picked up his paper and finished reading the Truman article. He drained his drink and went back to the bar to order another. He was careful to keep his distances from the Mob bunch.

The bartender gave him a warning glance that he pretended not to see.

One more double whiskey and if Vivian didn't show up, Tom would call it a night. It was useful to know the goons patronized the bar. The bosses might stay out of sight and order from room service, but they didn't confine their crew to the upstairs suites.

And the crew was restless. A curvy blonde in a green satin shift that was a stitch away from bursting at the seams was taking an interest in him. Tom kept his eyes on the paper but couldn't ignore the movement in his peripheral vision. The woman slipped from her barstool and ambled toward his shadowy retreat.

One of the bodyguards growled. "Billie, behave!"

"Fuck you," she snapped.

She must be one of the top squeezes or she would have been yanked back with a sharp tug on the leash. The guy in charge of her couldn't lay hands on her, so he followed, a calibrated two steps behind.

Interesting situation. The lady was bulletproof, but Tom wasn't. Nothing prevented the gorilla from swinging at him and rearranging his cervical vertebrae.

"Hey, sweetheart," she drawled.

Tom looked up from the paper. She sat on the arm of the chair Mark Jorgenson had vacated, showing so much smooth leg he could see the pale skin of her thigh above the nylon stocking. Promising, but not as good as Vivian or Rachel. He had built-in immunity.

"You're with the soap peddlers?"

He smiled. "Perfume mostly. And lipsticks." He leaned back in his chair, careful to look at her face, not her generous cleavage or exposed crotch. "Do you know we produce two hundred and fifty lipsticks every minute, round the clock?"

Her eyes went wide. "Golly, mister. You got any samples in your room?"

"Knock it off, Billie," the bodyguard said. "He's as queer as a three-dollar bill."

Tom stood up, gave her a little bow. "I won't argue about that. I like my job. And my face. Two hundred and fifty hot red tubes a minute. Imagine that, sweetheart. Goodnight." He touched the brim of his hat.

As he stepped toward the door, he saw Vivian and one of her escorts come toward him.

She blinked and dipped her chin.

Contact made. Now he had to catch her alone. The hotel didn't lack dark corners.

14. Monday, May 5

The hotel bed was big and soft. Abati left Vivian alone that night; he wasn't feeling well. Too much booze, probably. She got up after he went down to breakfast, took a long bath, and dressed in a comfortable skirt and silk blouse. The fabric would help her stay cool in this godforsaken climate. Much in need of coffee, she opened the door and found Aldo waiting.

"How long have you been standing there?"

"Since Mike went down."

"Jesus Christ. Next time come inside and sit on the sofa. You must look like an idiot waiting around out here. What will the other guests think?"

"All the bosses have guys in front of their doors. I didn't want to disturb you."

"Don't be silly. I was just getting dressed. How would your presence bother me?" She watched him blush. She poked the end of his nose. "It's sweet that I disturb you. Let's get some breakfast."

"Yes, ma'am."

Vivian ordered a fried egg on wheat toast, one piece of bacon, and a bowl of fruit. Abati and Leo weren't around. They must have moved on to meetings. Aldo gobbled down a large stack of pancakes under the interested eyes of tough guys and molls in their finest summer dresses.

"All those pancakes are going to make you fat, young man."

"I like pancakes." He swiped a forkful through a lake of maple syrup.

"Don't say I didn't warn you."

Vivian had burped, delicately, her fist pressed above her bosom, pinky extended, when an elegantly dressed man walked into the restaurant with two thugs and two blondes. The blondes were more interesting than the interchangeable hoodlums. One girl was thin and young, with small breasts and narrow hips, freckles and a bobbed haircut. She looked like one of those flapper creatures from the 1920s in a loose blue gown that draped her lean frame. The other blonde was a bombshell, with shiny hair in waves, and perfect curves in all the right places. The room went silent as the man pulled out a chair for each of his companions.

"Who is that?" Vivian muttered.

"Sam Giancana. He got in late last night. He's a big boss, Queenie. Don't stare at him. He won't like it."

"I wasn't staring at *him*." Vivian remembered seeing the hot number in the bar last night, close to Tom. Who was smiling.

"Oh, the va-va-voom blonde. That's Billie. I don't know the scrawny kid. First time I seen her."

Aldo told the waiter to charge their breakfast to Abati's room. He helped Vivian to her feet.

"Thank you, my good man. How about an outdoor ramble after such a filling repast?" She patted her belly. "We can survey the genteel grounds while the air is cool enough to inhale without scalding our lungs."

"Why are you talking like a book?"

"Am I? Do you read books?"

"No. But I like to walk. There's a rose garden in the back. The girl in the cigar shop told me they were in full bloom. The irises, too. Irises are my favorite flowers. The blossoms look like flames of color on long candle stalks, right before they open."

Vivian took Aldo's arm. "You're a strange kid."

After strolling through the gardens in the heavy morning air, learning all about irises and the coming dahlias, Vivian steered Aldo back toward the hotel. They crossed the side parking lot and a black Eldorado with Missouri plates almost ran into them. As they neared the hotel door, they saw Billie, Sam Giancana's curvy blonde, come out in a hurry. She waved at the Eldorado. The car stopped and the driver rolled his window down. She dropped an envelope onto the driver's lap. They talked briefly and the Eldorado roared away.

Billie turned back toward the hotel. She stopped in front of Vivian and appraised her outfit. She cocked her head. "I don't know you. Who are you with?"

"Mike Abati, San Francisco," said Vivian.

"Don't recall him. San Francisco, huh? Too cold for my blood." She shivered comically as she trotted toward the lobby, forearms covering her breasts.

"What a nut. Who was that in the Caddy?"

"Gizzo's driver. The Kansas City boss. He organized this whole thing. Billie met Mike at the last meeting, but you know blondes, they're scatter-brained."

"I'm a blonde sometimes," said Vivian. "If the spirit moves me and the money's right."

Aldo laughed. "But you're smart."

*

Tom called Gordon at FBI headquarters first thing in the morning. He gave him a quick status overview. He was in place at The Elms and he saw his girl, but she was closely watched. The big shots were on site, as the expensive vehicles in the parking lot showed, but so far Tom hadn't seen them in the common hotel areas. Gordon confirmed that the FBI had eyes on the bosses. Sunday's activities had taken place outside of the hotel, at the opening of the Cattle Show. Giancana and Trafficante hadn't been with the circus in town. Their four-car convoy was spotted arriving late in the evening.

"They rented a bus," Gordon said. "A brand-new thing with all the comforts. It'll be easier to keep track of them. All the cab hopping drives our guys crazy. We have men on the access roads to The Elms. We know who goes in and out."

"They should shift into business mode," Tom said, "and confine their activities to the hotel. I'll be in touch."

He walked the grounds after breakfast and saw the bus in the parking lot. Bodyguards patrolled the property, giving him a cold eye. The gangsters were not stupid. They knew that cops watched from the wings. Tom made a point of wearing his Avon badge. It wouldn't stop a bullet but it might give him the benefit of the doubt.

The morning agenda for the Avon conference featured guest speakers and product demonstrations. The delegates would get an exclusive look at exciting developments. Tom sat in the back and listened to the first presentation, that was both training and pep rally. The question time was lively. It made for enjoyable people watching. At the coffee break, he chatted with Mark Jorgenson, who asked him how the evening with the meat guys ended.

"I didn't stay long," Tom said. "I had another drink and called it a night. You have to give the pack space to roam, or they turn aggressive."

"You won't have that problem in here, quite the opposite. Our get-togethers are all about getting together."

"I enjoyed the presentation on selling techniques and network building." Tom was genuinely interested. "The club spirit. There must be an ideal customer group size. Too big becomes unwieldy."

Jorgenson smiled. "You're sure you don't want to move to sales? Most of our managers come from the field. They started with running groups. You need to be good with people, lots of empathy. I'm a numbers guy. I can't do it."

Tom didn't tell him that a good interrogator needed the same qualities. It made him look at the women in the room differently. They had an easy demeanor that was engaging. Not shy, not snobby, attractive without being intimidating.

"Have you had to tell some of them 'sorry, this isn't a job for you'?"

"The screening interviews are thorough, and then there's the results. It's easy to see who's good at it. Many think it'll be piece of cake and it's anything but."

Tom patted Jorgenson's shoulder. "I need a smoke. I'll see you later."

The restaurant was empty, except for two women, a thin blonde with long straight hair and a brown-skinned beauty who sent electricity through Tom's nerves with her direct stare. They were not Avon ladies.

In the main hallway Tom walked by a man in a black suit who must belong to the thug contingent, but otherwise the place was quiet. He didn't go near the meeting rooms in the west wing where most of the Mob activity was concentrated and explored the spa area. A man was swimming laps in the indoor pool. It seemed like a good way to spend an hour. Tom hadn't packed swim trunks. How could he have guessed he would end at a resort? A place like The Elms would have a shop with sport and leisure wear. Overpriced, no doubt.

The spa was big and luxurious. You could get a massage, sweat in a steam room, take ballet classes, even hit a bag and lift weights. Really nice. All that was missing was a shooting range. The goons would enjoy that. Spread some lead. A tearoom offered an array of pastries that made Tom's mouth water. The outdoor pool was behind a wall of French doors, with cushy chaises longues and parasols. And there was a shop, with clothes and jewelry. You didn't need to go to KC to blow yours or somebody else's bank account.

The shop girl flashed him a white-toothed smile.

"Good morning, sir. May I help you?"

"Your swimming pool is tempting but I didn't pack anything suitable."

She glanced at his Avon badge. "People come for a business meeting and forget we have a lot more to offer than conference rooms. Let me show you. This is the beginning of the season, and we have wonderful new arrivals, the latest California trends, for both men and women."

She didn't say boys and girls and Tom appreciated. This was awkward enough. He hated shopping for anything else than booze and cigarettes.

The shop was a lot bigger than the front led to believe. The men's area was all about sports, with golf and tennis attire on top of swim gear.

The girl pointed at a rack of colorful shirts and shorts. "Coordinates are very much in fashion this year, tropical prints especially." She must have seen Tom's eyebrows go up because she added, "pieces can be bought separately. Feel free to mix and match." She pointed at a door in the back. "The fitting rooms. Let me know if you need anything."

With a smile, she trotted away, leaving Tom in deep thought.

He wasn't a parrots, flamingos, and palm trees guy, which eliminated three quarters of the wares on display. He picked black swim trunks that looked the right size and a short-sleeved shirt with shadowy copper-colored leaves.

Perfect fit. Not cheap. He brought his picks to the counter.

"What do you suggest for footwear?" he said.

The girl considered him. "I don't see you in sandals, and you're too serious for Chucks. Tennis shoes would do but you chose dark colors … We have navy canvas, rubber soles, that would look nice. What's your shoe size?"

Tom felt positively decadent. This outing would make a dent in his wallet. He doubted Gordon, at the FBI, would cover the bill.

The girl was packing his purchases when he noticed movement by the door.

Vivian walked in with the splendid blonde from the bar—Billie, the muscle called her—and a busty redhead. They made a dazzling trio.

Billie saved him the trouble to try to get Vivian's attention.

"Hey, Avon man!" She turned to her companions. "This cute cookie was in the bar last night. You missed him, Queenie. Scrumptious bite." She came toward Tom, hips swaying beyond what body tolerance, or gravity, should allow.

"I should have swiped lipstick samples. Filled my pockets with goodies for you to snack on. What happened to your knight servant?"

She shrugged. "That mook. Doing his job, for a change." She pointed at the packages on the counter. "For you or your girl?"

Tom smiled. "I wanted to take a dip in the pool and I didn't have the gear."

She laughed, bawdy loud. "Oh baby, you got the gear!"

She was adorable. Tom winked. "Would be fun to meet you under the umbrellas."

"Planning to." She poked him in the chest. "See ya. Come on, girls, let's spend some of the company's dough."

She led the way through the racks of poolside dresses and bathing suits. The redhead followed. Vivian only pretended to and slipped to the side, behind the golf display.

Tom picked up his packages and thanked the shop girl who was soon hurrying after Billie, smelling a profitable sale.

Tom slinked toward the golf clubs. "What's the deal? I was at Union Station to get you out of this."

Vivian dipped behind the clothes racks. "There's a killer in town. He was on the train from L.A., Donato Gomma, the Eraser. He's good, Tommy, one of the best in the trade. It's a hit and it has to be big. Gomma is expensive."

"Truman?"

"That's what I'm thinking. I was at the grand opening of the cattle show last night. Bright lights and barbecue. Bunting everywhere. I didn't spot Gomma in the crowd and nothing happened during the speech, but that doesn't mean Truman isn't the target. There was a lot of security around him in a closed space. And I heard he'll be in town a bit longer. Plenty of time for Gomma to find an opening. After the speech we all piled into a bus and rolled over to hear Sinatra warble at a private gig for his Mob buddies. In the Drum Lounge, at the President Hotel. That's where I saw Gomma again. He was checking in. President Hotel. Truman. Get it?"

"I didn't think hired killers had a funny bone."

"I don't make you laugh sometimes?"

"You're special. Where's your chaperone?"

"Around. Not far."

Vivian drifted away to examine a selection of men's underpants. Tom sidled over and squatted with his knees below the shelf, hidden from the door. Vivian kept talking.

"After giving me the business with his eyes all evening, Sinatra announced that he had a couple shows lined up for the public this week. Not a surprise, but when I took a break at Abati's table I overheard goons talking about Frankie the Snitch. Seems he offered himself up to the feds a while back. He could be a target, too. They made a bet on when he'd find a bullet."

"Sinatra would be a side job for an expert hitman. Not the main act. He's not worth the price."

"The three molls I was sitting with had all gone the distance with him. Seems like he's making upstanding Mob connections wherever he performs. Who knows what he overhears and might want to sell. I thought he was going to hop off the stage and proposition me."

"Have you seen his current wife? Are you surprised?"

"I'm a better actress and he's not my type." She bumped her hip into Tom's head.

"What does Gomma look like?"

"Tall. Thin. Completely bald. Bright pink head."

"The Eraser. I get it."

"And you think we don't have a sense of humor."

"How come you know him?"

"I was hired to take him out after the Bugsy Siegel hit. He left the country before I could collect. The contract might still be open. With your permission, I could ..."

"As if you need my permission. How can you be sure he's here for business?"

"That would be one hell of a coincidence. Gomma has to be connected. To Truman or the Mob meeting, or both. Or Sinatra, who's only a breath away from the Mob meeting. He's not here for the cows, that's for sure."

"All right, good work. Let's get you out of here. I have a car."

She shook her head. "I can give you more, Tom. I'm in. Abati likes me."

"Viv, it's stupid and dangerous." Not to mention, completely unnecessary, but this wasn't the time and place to tell her that the FBI had pulled the plug on the operation.

"I was hired to find out what the meeting's all about. We don't know yet, do we?"

"You're giving us Gomma, a notorious assassin who might be planning to shoot the President. That's a lot more important than whatever the gangsters are cobbling together. What if Gomma recognizes you?"

"He saw me on the train. He didn't know who I was."

Tom sighed. "Ever thought you might be overconfident? You've been in this racket for years. You're not bulletproof, Vivian. There are more guns in this hotel than on Omaha Beach, and a platoon of guys who'll use them without a second thought."

"Don't patronize me, flatfoot." She turned her back on him. "Abati is dragging me back to the cattle show after lunch. You might tag along and learn something. I plan to buy a bathing suit. Wear good sunglasses, buddy boy. I'm gonna blind you."

He chuckled. Damn, she was a handful. "I'm in room four twenty-six. Where are you?"

"Three eighteen. The bodyguards share three twenty, when they're allowed to sleep. There's always one of them in front of our door if we're home." She bent down to kiss his forehead and hopped to the back of the store and Billie's bright laughter.

Tom had to see Gordon. Donato Gomma at the President Hotel deserved more than a phone conversation.

*

Ben Williams's Dodge Coronet was a glorious ride. It swallowed the miles back to town as eagerly as a horse kept in the barn too long.

The FBI command post was less hectic, with pauses between phone rings. Gordon was in a meeting. It must not have been important because he came out of it as soon as he saw Tom making hand signals through the glass door.

"We just talked," Gordon said. "You have something new?"

"I know why my girl decided to stay on the job. There's a killer in town."

Gordon pointed at the board with the Mob snapshots. "More than one."

"A contract killer named Donato Gomma, aka the Eraser. Ever heard of him?"

"He might have plugged Bugsy Siegel. The girl knows him?"

Tom had used the time on the road to concoct a vague cover story. "She overheard Mike Abati's bodyguards on the train. They were talking about the guy, and she saw him get off at the station. Then last night, she saw him again, at the President Hotel, he was checking in."

Gordon filled a cup of coffee from a carafe. "Jesus." He sipped, deep in thought. "She described him to you?"

Tom repeated Vivian's brief portrait. "The guy isn't in KC for the rodeo."

Gordon shook his head. "I'll take care of it right away. This is serious. The President is still doing the rounds."

"Gomma could also be in town for one of the Mob bosses, a repeat of the Siegel hit," Tom said.

"Pretty reckless to show himself to Abati's men."

"Mike Abati was not supposed to be on that train. By the way, Sinatra serenaded the mobsters last night. A couple of goons made bets on when he might be mowed down. They called him a snitch. Said he went to your boss offering candy. I doubt Gomma would be here for Frankie but he might be part of the package."

Gordon's eyes went wide. "The woman heard that too?"

"These heavies are regular chatterboxes."

He didn't add that the gangsters, like the FBI, thought the women were of no importance. They had no qualms babbling in front of them. They only paid attention to them in bed, and even then he doubted they really looked at them. If he ever had to run an undercover outfit he would staff it with the likes of Billie and Vivian. And take his cues from Avon. The people over there knew what they were doing.

"Is Truman leaving soon?" Tom said.

"The presidential schedule is confidential."

With the feds information sharing was strictly one way. As soon as the Eraser was neutralized Tom would pull Vivian out, kicks and screams be damned.

"Will you at least let me know when you have Gomma?"

Gordon made a face. "It's irregular ... yeah, all right. I'll leave a message at the hotel."

"I hate to bring it up but I'm running low on cash. Didn't expect to be staying at a resort for millionaires." He felt like a kid asking for money from his dad after blowing his allowance.

"Maybe stop buying drinks for all the lonely Avon ladies you want to tumble." Tom's hard face and tight mouth made Gordon take a quick breath. "Sorry. Bad joke. Stop at Personnel on your way out. Have them call me. I'll cut loose some dough. And thank your girl for the Gomma tip."

*

The thug wagon carried the Mob leadership back into town after lunch. Most of the molls remained at The Elms to work on their tans by the pool. Vivian and Muriel were among the handful drafted for the trip.

Vivian sat next to Abati on the ride and plied him with drinks from the bar, with a seasoning of heavy petting. When he started to feel mellow, she casually mentioned wanting to call her sister.

"I don't want to do it without your permission," she said. "I'm not used to meetings like these. If there's rules, and such."

He shrugged. "Yeah, like you know stuff to go sell to the cops ..." He raised a warning finger. "Don't call from the room. I know how you chicks yack for hours. Long distance, you'd ruin me."

After being introduced to a representative from a Texas cattle company, the cohort moved off to look at cows, and the women who had come along for the ride were released to explore the carnival. Vivian was under Aldo's supervision, as usual. The kid didn't mind. He was having fun. Muriel hung close to Vivian as they wandered along the colorful arcade. Their presence made it brighter. Aldo stopped at a shooting gallery to show off his prowess. The girls ignored him and slipped away.

Muriel tapped Vivian on the shoulder.

"The guy you flirted with at the gift shop is following us. He's a hunk, if you ask me, but he'd better be careful if he values his sharp profile. We got eyes on our rumps."

Muriel had noticed Tom and Vivian's private moment. The girl was more observant than she appeared.

"USDA Prime rumps, my dear. And Aldo's eyes are on his target practice. Where is this guy?" Vivian made a shade of her hand under the blazing sun.

Muriel pointed with her strawberry ice cream cone. Vivian could see Tom now. The brim of his hat shaded his features, and her heart beat a little faster, as it always did when she looked at him. She loved the tilt he gave to that gray fedora. Vivian worked her tongue over her ice cream cone, and the melting vanilla dripped over her fingers. A newsreel cameraman walked by, his machine storing memories of the festive afternoon. He stopped and captured Vivian licking the cream from her fingers. It was a pretty picture. She performed the act as provocatively as she could while the film rolled and the cameraman leered, a toothy grin on his thin face. No respectable production company would ever show that suggestive piece of film.

Vivian strolled up to Tom. He stood at the counter of a ring toss game. She leaned over the counter, pretending to look for something in the sawdust. The camera was still whirring behind her. She didn't have to turn to know the photographer zoomed on her backside.

She kept her voice low. "Glad you made it."

He laid down a dime, and the carny handed him three wooden rings. She licked at her cone and Tom missed the milk bottles with all three tosses.

"Try your luck again, sir?" the carny asked. Tom shook his head.

"The redhead is watching us," he muttered.

"Should I strangle her behind the penny pitch?"

"I passed your information on to the feds. They said they would nab Gomma. Once he's out of contention, we're out of here."

"I saw Billie having lunch with Anthony Gizzo today. You know Billie, right? Blonde, more curves than an ace pitcher. She seems to have a cavity-inducing sweet spot for you." She gave another long lick at the ice cream cone. "Anyway, it was a heated discussion. Gizzo is single here. Wouldn't it be funny if he had a crush on Sam Giancana's lady? Mind you, Sam has another bed-warmer at hand, a wispy thing, flat as a board. Who would have thought Mob meetings were that packed with romance. And as if there weren't enough cherries on the cake, the bosses are meeting with people from a Texas ranch, as we speak. Strange things are cooking, Tommy."

"Jesus, Viv, it isn't a game, you …"

"Queenie!" Aldo had found her.

Vivian turned away from Tom and waved at Aldo. Tom laid another dime on the counter and was handed three more rings. He missed with all of them again. Vivian took Aldo's arm and pulled him back toward Muriel, a smile on her face at Tom's continued bad luck.

The big shots talked cattle, or so it seemed, all afternoon. Out of sight. The carnival was a mixture of pleasant and disgusting smells. Pork ribs and a child's vomit. Vivian consumed a hamburger after the ice-cream cone. Muriel insisted on buying her a coke, but what she really wanted was a proper Old Fashioned. With two cherries. The redhead had come out of her shell as they spent time together wandering back and forth in front of the carnies with a cheerful Aldo.

Vivian pointed at a row of phone booths lined against one of the exhibition buildings. "I asked Mike," she said. "He has no problem with me calling my sister." She punched Aldo's chest playfully. "Give me five minutes, kid. Keep Muriel company, will you?"

The number for her Commie contact in Kansas City was branded in her memory.

The man picked up immediately. He didn't volunteer a name, just a: "Yes?"

"I'm calling about the downtown meeting tomorrow afternoon," Vivian said.

"The meeting has been cancelled. He's gone."

She gripped the handset harder. "What?"

"From what I heard, he was hauled away in a hurry. My source said the security guys freaked out and sent him home. No warning, no reason given."

"You're sure?" As soon as she asked, she felt stupid. Of course, he was sure.

"Better luck next time."

"What if I'm not available next time."

"You were paid an extraordinary fee up front. We'll be in touch." He hung up.

"We'll see about that," said Vivian.

She took a deep breath. It was a strange feeling, like standing at the exact moment in time when day turns into night, neither one nor the other, a light switch frozen in-between. Truman had left town unexpectedly. The contract had evaporated. For now.

And she was relieved, light-headed.

She stood in the phone booth, holding the handset, grateful for the glass walls of the box that helped her stay upright, in a bubble of silence that would burst when she opened the door. She waited for what seemed like a long time and might have been a minute. If that.

She stepped out. The ground didn't feel as solid as it should and she stamped a foot to make it real again.

"Are you all right?" Muriel said.

"Yes. I …" Vivian remembered the excuse for the call. "My sister … she's going to have a baby."

Muriel jumped, clapping in joy. "You're going to be an aunt! That's wonderful! Isn't it wonderful, Aldo?"

The kid looked stumped. "Yeah, I guess."

Vivian laughed. "I'm with you. Diapers, milk bottles, sleepless nights. Just thinking about it makes me want to have a drink. Let's go have fun, children."

They resumed their lazy strolling along the midway. Muriel drank coca cola like it was water and Vivian was dying of a different kind of thirst.

The redhead insisted until Vivian agreed to take a spin with her on the Ferris wheel. Aldo went pale at the thought, and said he'd watch the girls from below. Once on, they couldn't go anywhere anyway.

After the third spin around, Vivian was bored, but the view of the river and the city wasn't bad and the fresh air was a relief. The motion was soothing. Until the rickety machine ground to a halt with Vivian and Muriel at the very top.

"Aw, shit," said Vivian.

The machine's gears screamed as they attempted to get rolling again. Black smoke poured out of the diesel engine. The noise was ear-splitting.

"What's going on?" Muriel said. "Goddamnit, I have to pee."

People screamed. Children wailed. Folks on the ground pointed into the air and shouted. The guy running the machine stood in his greasy coveralls and scratched his head. It was a crazy cattle show all its own.

"I'm scared," Muriel said.

"Should we climb down?"

"Are you nuts!"

"Just kidding." Vivian looked down. She had climbed worse.

"I wanna go home. I hate these business trips."

"Why do you come?"

"Because Joey will beat the shit out of me if I don't."

"Maybe you should tell him to go to hell. Maybe you should leave. Do you think he'd spend much time looking for you if you slipped away?"

"He knows where I come from. My family. He'd take it out on them."

"I doubt he'd bother. Go west. You can get lost out there. That's what I did."

"My family needs the money Joey lets me send them. I can't quit mom and pop just like that."

"I'm sure they're proud of their little girl. Where did you grow up?" Vivian had to keep the girl distracted. A panicked kid in a swinging gondola was bad news.

"Plainview. Left home at sixteen and got a modelling job in Dallas. Joey found me soon after. Maybe I'll never get out."

Muriel was fidgety. She kept her eyes on her shoes and avoided looking at the empty air all around them. Vivian put an arm around the girl's waist. What the hell were they waiting for down there?

"I imagine it's hard when you have family to care for. I left home at seventeen, but I was alone by then. My mom and pop had died. My stepfather too, the lousy shitbag. I'll never go back to Idaho. There's nothing good to remember about that god-forsaken place."

Muriel's head dropped onto Vivian's shoulder. "I'm scared."

"We'll be down soon. This wheel isn't going to come loose and roll away." Oh shit, why did she put that thought in the girl's head? And why had Muriel insisted on riding this thing if she was acting like a little girl scared of heights? To talk in private?

"I did something bad."

Bingo.

Vivian looked down the spoke. It wasn't that scary. They weren't that high. This was a measly Ferris wheel.

"You want to tell me about it?"

"I can't."

A late afternoon breeze licked at their hair. The sun wouldn't quit, but it had moved behind them, out of their eyes. Banging and clanging sounds rose up from below. A collection of carnies and know-it-alls shouted at each other like damned fools. Abati and the other bosses showed up and joined in the mayhem. Vivian saw Abati slap Aldo in the side of the head, knocking his fedora off, as if he was responsible for the wheel being stuck.

"Now I've peed my pants," Muriel said, tears in her eyes. "I'm all wet."

"That's okay, hon. No one will know." Vivian removed a wad of Kleenex from her pocket and handed it to Muriel. The breeze killed the smell of urine. And the stockyards. And all the crap below them that looked pitiful. "Take your pants off and set them on the seat. The sun will dry everything in no time. I'll be right back."

Muriel's eyes widened. "Where are you going?"

"Down to find out what's up." Vivian slipped off her oxfords and climbed over the edge of the wavering gondola.

"I can't watch that," said Muriel. "I'm gonna be sick."

"I'll be right back. And I'll tell you about my stunts in Hollywood."

Vivian held onto the drive rim. She gripped the long spoke and slid down to the wheel support. Grease soon covered the front of her sundress. People trapped in surrounding gondolas cheered as she rested in the middle of the great wheel, like a butterfly on a steel porch chair. With a deep breath, she slithered down one of the lateral support arms until she was ten feet off the ground. Mike Abati glared at her.

"Come here, Queenie. We need to go to dinner."

That's what he was thinking about? Dinner? She wanted to hit him on the head. Harder than he slapped Aldo. "I'm not leaving Muriel up there."

Piranio pushed his way past Abati. "I'll put a scare into her. What do you dames think you're doing? We don't have time for this nonsense."

Vivian was fuming. "So, it's our fault now? We didn't

break the damn Ferris wheel. It was supposed to be a simple ride. Up and down and all around for sightseeing and a bit of a breeze. We're your girls, and we're in danger. It wouldn't kill you to show a little concern."

"Are you going to give her a whipping, Mike, or should I?"

"I take care of my own. Get your ass over here, Queenie."

"Muriel is up there, you big ape." Vivian shinnied back up the arm to the wheel support. She heard Aldo pipe up.

"I couldn't do that climb. She's like a monkey."

"You can't do anything, you jackass," said Abati. "Why did you let them go up there?"

"There was no harm in it."

Abati whacked Aldo in the side of the head again. After pulling herself up the spoke, Vivian grabbed the support and flopped into the gondola to the cheering of the other stranded passengers.

"Golly, Vivian. You're strong as a man," said Muriel.

"Not as strong as I used to be." She was drenched in sweat, her breath coming hard.

The machine lurched to life a few minutes later, making some people scream in fear at the sudden jolt. Muriel slipped on her underpants, and in no time, they were being berated by angry mobsters on solid ground.

"You two numbskulls have made us all late for dinner," said Abati. "Now the boys are hungry."

"I'm thirsty," Vivian said. "I wouldn't mind a stiff cocktail."

"Look at the front of your dress. I can't take you into a restaurant looking like that."

"You're Mike Abati. Bay Area Big Shot. You can do whatever you want." She took his arm and whispered something about handcuffs into his ear.

"All right." Piranio booted Muriel in the rear. "The Golden Ox is right around the corner at the Livestock Exchange. I could use a good steak after listening to those wax-borers go on and on about Mexican cattle all day."

He pushed Muriel in the back, and she stumbled to her knees. When Vivian moved toward the fallen girl, Abati grabbed her arm. She turned to him, and he shook his head.

Vivian had a last look at the wheel. Tom was right there, leaning on the fence, tall and straight against the backdrop of the spokes, clean looking in his gray suit, a lot cleaner than she was. He shot her a lopsided smile and lit a cigarette.

She could hear his voice in her head.

"Good show, girl." And then. "What did that get you?"

15. Tuesday, May 6

There was no message from Gordon in the morning, and the federal agent did not pick up the phone when Tom called. If he wanted news, he'd have to drive to Kansas City. He suspected the news wasn't good. Unless what happened was so important that it couldn't be shared with a lowly San Francisco homicide detective.

Before engaging in a shouting match with the feds, Tom decided to call Rachel. She must be on tenterhooks.

He caught her at the *Chronicle.*

"I've been thinking about you." She kept her voice flat but there was a definite hint of reproach in there.

"I'm sorry honey, something happened." And he couldn't share with her. "I feel like I'm benched." A better analogy was that he'd been recruited by a great team that used his game plans but didn't give him anything to do. "Lots of time wasted waiting for other people to do their job." He shrugged. "How are you doing?"

"I'm on a nasty kidnapping case," Rachel said. "You haven't heard anything where you are?"

"The paper here is full of …" He chuckled. "Ah, nice try!"

She laughed. "One day, I'll trip you up. The twelve-year-old daughter of a state rep has been abducted. It seems professional. There's a cryptic ransom note. Your boss is holding a press conference this morning. The FBI is plugged in."

Tom wondered if Burdon and Stansted were on call. "Good luck with that. They like to play it close to the vest."

"I'm sure you have stories. Okay, I won't do that again. Do you have a new travel date?"

"End of the week for sure, but I'm trying to get out of it sooner. I love you, darling."

"Be careful, Tom."

It made him feel a little better. He resisted calling Pete Delgado. To tell him what? That the whole thing was a side plot? All his friend would say was *I knew it*.

Tom called to get the gray suit pressed and a couple shirts laundered and drove to Kansas City. Where a surprise awaited him.

The FBI command post was being dismantled. No wonder his call went nowhere. The phone bank with the busy ladies was gone. A few agents were still around, stashing documents in boxes. One of them was removing the mobsters' photo gallery from the display boards.

Tom grabbed him by the arm. "You guys are leaving?"

"What do you think?" And he was gone, with his stack of photos.

Gordon was near the large city map, collecting push pins.

"Ah, Keegan, good of you to come."

Good? As if he'd been invited to give a hand at the bake sale. "What about the message you were supposed to leave at The Elms. You nailed Gomma?"

Gordon shook his head. "He was gone. Stayed one night and checked out."

"Goddamnit, you missed him. You're telling me he's in the wind?"

"Why do you think we're leaving? Truman's back in DC. We weren't going to have him out there, exposed, with Gomma gunning for him. I wish we'd nailed the man, but the President is our priority and he's safe. Thanks to you and your girl."

Tom shrugged off the casual praise. "Has Gomma been spotted at the train station? Anywhere?"

"We put out a bulletin. His description has been distributed to every law enforcement agency. He'll be caught."

Tom pulled out his cigarettes and lit up. He didn't offer one to Gordon. "What about your people undercover at The Elms?"

"They've been recalled."

"No eyes on the Mob convention?"

"Local law enforcement is taking over. They'll make

sure these guys don't cause any ruckus."

"I'm sure the local constable will ticket them for traffic violations. Can't catch them for drunk driving, they travel by bus. Have a safe trip back to DC. My regards to J. Edgar."

Tom turned on his heels. Gomma being somewhere out there didn't sit right with him. The President was gone and he was the high-value target, but the Eraser had done work for gangsters before. Who was to say, he wasn't in town for a similar hit? Innocent civilians were at The Elms with a bunch of trigger-happy goons. If bullets started to fly …

Gordon said the local cops were in charge. Tom found an officer on the ground floor of the courthouse and asked for directions. Police HQ was around the corner, at Locust and 12th.

The FBI had packed but the KC cops were still in full rodeo mode and clocking overtime. A homicide detective was at his desk and gave Tom a warm welcome. He didn't bring him a dead body, and that was appreciated.

Detective Campbell knew about the gathering at The Elms. The local cops were fully engaged. At least, the feds had not kept them in the dark.

"You're inside?" Campbell said. "They're behaving?"

"The muscle seems to be satisfied with looking menacing. I'm here because something worries me."

Campbell had seen the bulletin about Donato Gomma, with the man's description.

"Maybe he left town but nobody has seen him since he checked out of the President Hotel. Why did he come to KC? It could have been for Truman, but Gomma has Mob connections. He took out Bugsy Siegel in '47. Now that the President has left, the big potential targets are at The Elms."

Campbell pondered. "The best outcome is we locate him and set up surveillance. We grab him when there's no danger for civilians. I agree with you that The Elms is the place to watch, and it's a powder keg. The good news is that we're on the ball already. We've been keeping an eye on the heavies since they rolled into town. From a distance, no confrontation.

We're in position on the access roads to the resort. And now that the undercover feds have vacated the premises, we're moving our people inside. I'll make sure they're briefed."

Tom nodded. "Anybody I can go to if needed?"

"My partner, Eric Robinson, is pretending to be the concierge's assistant. Tall, with a crew cut and a nose like a cattle chute." Campbell reached in a desk drawer and extracted a handful of cards. He scribbled something on the back. "Your credentials. Show that to Eric and the guys at the checkpoint that isn't a checkpoint." He winked. "If they've done their job well, you'll have to squint to spot them. They know how to set a deer blind."

Campbell had scribbled: *Give this guy a hand.* And signed Cy Campbell.

"You realize these are *get out of jail free* cards," Tom said.

"Yep. You're at The Elms for a reason, Keegan." He raised a hand. "Don't wanna know, but you're not with the feds, and that smells like a mystery."

"I have an asset in there who needs protection."

"Figured that much."

The guy was good. Tom slipped a card on the desk, in exchange for the signed deck. "If you're ever in San Francisco, give me a ring."

"Don't mind if I do." Campbell pushed up the drawl. "Your asset, she's an Avon lady?"

"No, but I made friends in that crowd. I'd hate to see them caught in the crossfire."

"Me too. Avon's a valued customer around here. Good business. Very little trouble."

"You know how many lipsticks they roll off the line every minute of the day?" Campbell raised a questioning eyebrow. "Two hundred and fifty."

Campbell laughed. "Holy smokes, gonna tell my wife!" He held out his hand. "Good luck, pal."

*

The handcuffs Vivian promised Abati to mollify him about the

Ferris wheel escapade had etched raw red rings around her wrists. She tried to rub the pain out of them at breakfast. Bacon helped, though that was going into her mouth. Vicki smirked at her over coffee. Aldo sat a few tables away, staring at her over the top of a newspaper. He must be wondering how the cuffs had been used. She was pleased to see that he held the tabloid right side up.

"I won't let my guy do that to me," said Vicki. "Not with my fair skin."

"I wouldn't, either." Jasmine smirked. "That's because I'm a real Queen."

"Yeah, I get it. I'm just a lowly rental. My guy doesn't give a shit about me."

"It's your life," said Jasmine. "Don't complain to me about it."

Abati had gone to work on her once they were back at The Elms. Everybody had gotten drunk at the Golden Ox. Passions were inflamed.

When Vivian emerged from the bathtub, Abati was snoring, flat on his back on the wide bed. She pulled on a pair of loose, red silk pants and matching blouse. Aldo was waiting outside the door, as expected. She dropped off her grease-stained dress with a hotel laundress and met Vicki and Jasmine in the restaurant.

"Are you going back into town today?" Vicki dipped her doughnut into well-creamed coffee.

"Not a chance," Vivian said. "I'm going to pour myself into a new swimsuit, step into the healing waters, and soak all my aches and pains away."

"I heard about your he-man antics on the Ferris wheel," said Jasmine. "You're insane. No offense."

"No offense taken. Have you seen Muriel this morning? Piranio was all over her yesterday."

"Here she comes," said Vicki. "Oh dear, look at the poor thing."

Muriel came to the table, a hand shading her left eye. The other eye was bloodshot.

"Sit." Jasmine stood up. "I'll get you some coffee."

The girl flopped into a seat and Vivian pulled Muriel's hand away from her eye. "Let me see it." The area was badly bruised. Purple. With greenish edges. Another bruise was starting to fill in around her jaw. "Jesus Christ."

"Jesus fucking Christ," said Vicki.

"That fucking Texas bastard." Jasmine returned with the coffee and sat next to Muriel.

"Good Heavens." An Avon lady in a well-tailored pink suit stopped at their table. She stared at Muriel's bruise. "Are you okay? Have you seen a doctor?"

"None of your fucking business," Jasmine said. "Go play with your lipstick."

"I was a nurse before I started playing with lipstick. May I take a look, Miss? I want to make sure your jaw isn't broken."

"She'd be screaming her head off if her jaw was broken. I told you to get lost." Jasmine rose from her seat.

"Let her take a look," Vivian said. "She's a nurse."

"*Was* a nurse." Jasmine sniggered.

"A surgical nurse." The woman set her purse on the table and knelt at Muriel's side. "How did this happen?"

No one spoke. Aldo had dropped his newspaper and moved closer. Vivian signaled him to stay away. The girls weren't in the mood to tolerate a male's presence.

"I've treated women who were beaten by their husbands. Is no one going to say anything?"

"Why did you quit being a nurse?" asked Vicki.

The girls leaned in as the woman gently manipulated Muriel's features. She pried Muriel's jaw open and looked at her teeth while Muriel gazed at the ceiling, wincing.

"My husband was an army doctor. He was killed near the end of the war. I needed to spend more time at home with my children, so I got into the door-to-door racket. I make a good living but I do miss my patients." She stood up and stroked Muriel's head. "Thank God your pretty nose isn't broken. May I sit? My name is June Cavendish. I have a proposition."

"Queenie is the one to talk to, then." Jasmine reached to her side to pull a chair over from the next table.

"What do you mean?" June sat and adjusted her skirt.

"She's calling me a whore without calling me a whore," Vivian said. "Subtle, like."

June eyed all the women in turn, the color of her skin rising. "What do you all do? You're part of the Italian cattleman convention?"

"Oh, yeah. We're the cattle," said Vicki.

June took a quick breath. "You're all so lovely. Each one of you in your own way."

"What's the proposition?" Jasmine asked.

"We're giving a demonstration of the new Avon products this afternoon. The reps will be handling the makeup and trying it out on themselves. We sometimes hire models for group demonstrations, but we don't have any this time around. Would you girls be willing to sit in as our models? You've all got different coloring. It would be delightful to have you. And you'll get all the free samples you can carry. The demonstration begins at one o'clock."

"Hot diggity," Vicki said. "Beats another stinking day at the stockyard."

"What's going on?" Billie walked up behind Muriel and slapped her on the back. Muriel nearly jumped out of her seat.

"Cattle call," Jasmine said. "We've been invited to participate in an Avon make-up demonstration. They need a herd of models, so we're being rounded up by this dame here."

"June Cavendish." She held her hand out to Billie. "I'm with Avon. Head of Advertising."

"Oh baby, I'll be there." Billie laughed. "With bells on."

"Rain check for me," said Vivian. "I'm buying a swimsuit. Should have gotten one yesterday. Muriel and I are going to spend the day in the pool. I don't want to see a single dark suit for a few hours, and I'm done with cows and barbecue. I've got my fill of KC. Muriel, come." She got up. Muriel followed her like a puppy.

Aldo joined the migration, staying a cautious few steps behind. As Vivian reached the door of the restaurant, June stopped her.

"Bring her to my room. I'll fix her face. When I'm done nobody will notice the bruises unless they're looking for them."

Aldo was now at Vivian's side. "This guy has to come with me," she said.

"To my room?"

"Everywhere but the potty. Right, Aldo?"

"Boss's orders, Queenie. You know that."

"Very well." June led them to her door in the east wing, unlocked it, and ushered everyone in.

"Thanks for doing this, June. I'm going to buy that swimsuit, and I'll take the boy with me. Give you some privacy." Vivian turned to Muriel. "Let's meet after lunch and soak while the other girls are getting their faces renovated. One o'clock. At the indoor pool."

Muriel nodded.

Aldo opened the door and stepped out with Vivian.

"I would never hit you," he said.

"You wouldn't live two minutes if you did."

The shop on the ground floor was not crowded. The cheerful woman who'd helped the girls the day before greeted Vivian and her security guard with a smile.

"Nice to see you again, ma'am. Your friend hasn't stopped back in. I guess he liked the look of his new leisure wear. How may I help you today?"

"I need a swimsuit." Vivian cut her eyes toward Aldo to see if the woman's unfortunate comments had resonated. They hadn't. "I prefer a one-piece."

"We carry Jantzen, Catalina, and Rose Marie Reid. We have a few of the new strapless outfits made from shirred acetate. What's your size?"

Vivian chose a baby-doll outfit by Catalina with shorts

rather than a skirt. White with vertical green stripes. The suit would cover her from thighs to cleavage, hiding a knife scar above her pelvis, and a line of scarred stiches below her right breast. Abati, despite his infatuation with her behind, hadn't noticed the dimple a .32 slug had made in her left buttock. He rarely wore his glasses to bed.

16. Tuesday, May 6

Muriel's sandals clacked along the edge of the steaming pool just as Vivian appeared in costume with Aldo. The shapely girl wore a white two-piece, and everyone sprawled in the area watched her bend over to set her things down. Aldo wore a tight pair of trunks and wore them well. Naked from the waist up, he offered a lot of well-built structure to look at. He dived, showing off his physical abilities, as soon as Vivian set down her towel and robe on a lounger.

"He looks good," Muriel said.

Her face was healthier thanks to June Cavendish's ministrations but there was swelling around the blue eyes. Vivian thought a bag of ice would be a better tonic than a soak in hot mineral springs.

"He's a good kid. With a big heart. A little dumb. A girl could do a lot worse."

"I could go for a dumb guy who treated me right."

Vivian raised her thumb in approval and slipped into the hot water. She could feel the minerals soothe her flesh. The heat felt good on her tender wrists. It had been a challenging few days but she enjoyed physical adventure and didn't consider her body a holy temple. Abati was easy to satisfy. He fell asleep all at once after sex and didn't bother her during the night. She closed her eyes and let the warmth envelop her. If an attendant came by, she would reserve a massage for her and Muriel, even Aldo. All together in the same room. Boss's orders.

The redhead dropped in beside her and murmured something unintelligible. Half moan, half sigh of pleasure. A red plastic ball floated by and Vivian picked it up. When Aldo splashed close, she threw it across the pool.

"Fetch."

Aldo smiled with all his strong white teeth on display and swam after it. Vivian turned to Muriel.

"What did you mean on the Ferris wheel when you said you did something bad?"

"I didn't mean anything."

"You can trust me, Muriel. What did you mean?"

"I can't say."

"I won't tell anyone, kid. I like you. I'll look after you."

"Joey would kill me if he found out."

"I'm a rented girl. I'm not part of this world. I don't care about any of these guys. They can rot in hell for all I care."

Muriel raised her pale eyes to Vivian. "I talked to the police."

"It's brave, but you shouldn't have done that. Officers of the law can be bought, honey. They'll talk for peanuts. You don't know who to trust. What did you tell them?"

The red ball splashed at Vivian's chest. Water stung her eyes. Aldo stood five feet away. Panting. Vivian grabbed the ball and threw high and far. Aldo crashed after it. He liked making waves, the bigger the better.

"I hate Joey. He says he loves me, but I don't believe it. I know he goes with other women, and he makes me go with his friends and business contacts." Muriel slid closer to Vivian along the wall. Their shoulders touched. "I want out, Queenie. I hate him and I hate my life. A guy stopped me on the street one day when I was shopping. A fed, I think. He said he could protect me and my family if I gave him information on Joey. I wanted out so bad … I said I would do it. One night I listened into a phone call from another room. Joey was talking to a cattle guy, in Texas. Some big shot. They were talking about a new breed of cow, and how they could bring it up from Mexico to Dallas. A Mexican Brown they called it. I heard them talk about these cows again, yesterday, after Joey punched me all black and blue."

"You told the feds about the cows?"

"Never had a chance, we left to come here a couple days later."

Vivian sighed. "Don't talk to the feds, or any cop, ever again, kid. They'll pump you for all you got and won't give you anything for it. Next time somebody stops you in the street, walk right by. You can get out of this thing with Piranio, but the cops are not the way, believe me."

The ball splashed in front of her face again. She retrieved it and threw it to the far end of the pool. She put everything she had in that throw, with rage on top.

Mexican Brown. Heroin. So that was what the bosses were doing among the herds. Dividing the heads of cattle, so to speak. It also explained why she hadn't seen Giancana and Trafficante downtown. They were at The Elms but kept to their suites in the hotel and the large meeting room on the ground floor. The two top guys wouldn't be seen negotiating with intermediaries at the rodeo, that was the job of the lower ranks. Vivian wished she had not been dragged to KC with the pack. The real business happened at The Elms. Maybe she should leave this pool and find a quiet corner near the meeting room, keep an eye on who went in and out of there to report to Sam and Sonny. Maybe put her ear to the door. Good luck doing that with Aldo on her ass.

"Who is he, Queenie?"

Muriel's voice pulled her out of her cogitations.

"What?"

"Is he your boyfriend or your pimp? Keeping an eye on you when you're working. For protection? If you're fucking that guy, I can't imagine how you tolerate Abati."

Vivian's eyes followed the direction Muriel pointed at with her chin.

On the other side of the pool, Tom was putting down a towel on a lounge chair. He dropped his shirt on the back of the lounger and kicked off his canvas shoes. He stood on the side of the pool and dove in, barely disturbing the water.

"Very smooth," Muriel said. "Makes you wish you had another ball to throw?"

*

Tom swam a couple of leisurely lengths. The water was too warm for real exercise and the mineral content felt strange on his skin but the prickly sensation wasn't unpleasant.

The pool wasn't crowded. Avon ladies occupied a cluster of chaises longues, taking a break from the conference.

On the other side, at a safe distance, a trio of Mob girlfriends were gathered under the supervision of a gorilla in a dark suit standing rigid like a statue against the back wall. He must be sweating gallons. Vivian and the redhead from the Ferris wheel floated in the pool with her assigned escort, the young man working for Mike Abati. He was goofing around. If his boss saw him, he would earn another volley of head slaps, to match those he received at the carnival. Two more couples splashed around, probably day visitors to the spa.

Tom couldn't see a way to approach Vivian without raising suspicion. He would have to catch her when she went back to the ladies dressing room, her handler wouldn't follow her in there. He was mapping the layout of the spa area in his mind when a big splash sent a wet wave in his face. A grinning Mark Jorgenson emerged in front of him.

"Hey, I'm not the only one playing hooky."

"You don't have sales duties today?" Tom said.

"They're doing make-up demonstrations in the conference room. Ooohs, aaahs, and lots of giggling. The girls are having a blast. Not much for me to do." He floated on his back, kicking lazily. "The view is pretty good from here."

"The pool ceiling?" Tom smiled.

Mark rolled around. "That is one yummy redhead. I think I'll go introduce myself."

"Careful, the girls have a chaperone, and looking at his shoulders, I'm sure he works with weights."

"Can't keep his six-shooter in his swim trunks."

"He'll dunk you with one hand behind his back."

"She's too cute. I'll take a chance."

Mark kicked his feet and aimed for Vivian and her friend. Tom followed slowly, keeping an eye on Abati's watchdog who was on the other side of the pool, in the vapors. When he reached Vivian, Mark was already chatting with the redhead. Her name was Muriel. Pretty. And she'd been worked over. The make-up job was first class, but Tom had seen too many battered women to be fooled by a layer of foundation. Mark, on the other hand, was unaware. The girl laughed, delighted. She was frightfully young. Twenty, if that.

Tom slipped to the side, creating distance. Vivian pushed herself up and sat on the edge of the pool, legs in the water. They were two feet apart.

"They missed Gomma," Tom muttered. "He wasn't at the hotel anymore."

"Damn. Where is he?"

"No idea. The feds have closed shop. They shipped Truman out after they bungled Gomma's arrest. We need to go, Viv. The game is up."

She leaned back on her elbows and stared at the ceiling. She had a strange expression on her face. Troubled, amused? Tom couldn't read her.

"I know what the meeting's for," she said. "Mexican Brown. Dope. The ranch and cow stuff is a cover. They're setting up delivery channels. Mexico to Dallas, to KC, to Chicago is my guess. Muriel was approached by the feds to snitch on Joey Piranio. I don't know what she told them. Nothing about the drugs. She heard Mexican Brown and thought it was a breed of cattle."

"Jesus." Tom let himself sink. The briefing with FBI agent Burdon. An informant in Texas told them the Mob was meeting in Kansas City. It looked like the redhead flirting with Mark Jorgenson was the source. She was the reason he was here. She was the reason Vivian was in Mike Abati's bed. Did Burdon lie when he said they needed eyes on the Mob gathering? They already had Muriel's. Didn't they trust the girl?

He came up for air in time to see Vivian throw a ball all the way to the end of the pool.

"Aldo likes to fetch," she said.

"The pup is bigger than a Saint Bernard. Piranio knows Muriel snitched? That's why she's all banged up?"

"He punished her for being stuck on the Ferris wheel with me and making the bosses late for dinner." Vivian shrugged. "Don't ask. The man is a beast. I agree, tomorrow we go, but Muriel comes with us. I can't leave her behind.

Piranio will kill her someday."

Aldo was swimming back, holding the ball aloft.

"Same time tomorrow, bring her here," Tom said.

He pulled himself out of the pool and walked away. He hoped Mark Jorgenson could take care of himself. He should be all right. Aldo was only tasked with keeping an eye on Vivian.

Tom didn't feel an urge to report back to anybody. The feds had left town. He didn't own them any loyalty. They jerked Vivian and him around. But he owed Pete Delgado a phone call, dope was his beat. Let him and the chief decide how much they wanted to tell the agents who sent them on this wild goose chase.

And he had to work on their exit strategy. Muriel was extra baggage. He trusted Vivian would handle her.

*

Tom did another slow walk around the sprawling resort. This time he didn't focus on the accesses to the hotel, but on the connections between the spa area and the rest of the facilities. The two public entrances were on both sides of the shop. There was a maintenance access on the corner of the outside pool, a wooden door painted green to match the hedge and bushes that surrounded the area and provided privacy. The lock was a simple one. He could pop it with a pocketknife. Better do that tomorrow around lunchtime. If he damaged the lock now, an employee might notice and put a padlock on the door.

He moved the Dodge to the rear parking lot that was next to the maintenance shed. It was all he could accomplish today. He grabbed a hamburger at the restaurant and peeked into the Avon conference room where cocktail time was getting under way. June Cavendish waved at him. It would be rude to ignore her.

"You haven't been very assiduous," she said.

"I enjoyed the presentations this morning. The job is the problem. I have to follow up on things. My telephone bill will be nasty. I expect my boss to haggle."

She smiled. "No rest for the wicked." She handed him

a glass of champagne.

"I took a dip in the pool this afternoon, during the make-up session. It was reviving. Have you tried it?"

"I swim laps every morning. While everybody's still in bed. It kicks me awake." She tilted her head. "Is the spa overrun by the meat conventioneers during the day?"

"A few rare birds. They're not much into healthy or sporty pursuits," Tom said.

"Except boxing." She made a face. "I fixed one of their girls today. She refused to tell me who did it. I swear I would have called the police on that animal. We help women in the company. We help them get financially independent. It seems minor compared to what that girl has to deal with."

"You can't save everybody, June."

"I wish I was a man. I would punch that guy in the face, like he did to her. Make him feel the pain. Then, maybe he'd understand." She stared at him.

Tom took his cigarettes out and lit one. "It's tempting to respond to violence with violence. There are better ways."

"With people like that, I doubt it." She turned on her heel and left.

Tom drained his drink, and it made him want another one. Something with more of a kick. He'd disappointed June. Why it left him with a bad taste in the mouth, he wasn't sure.

*

The hotel bar was packed with giggling girls. None of them belonged to the Avon contingent. They crowded Mark Jorgenson who was holding court behind a box full of lipsticks and lotions. The redhead, Muriel, was eating him up with her big blue eyes. If he were a slice of cake, he wouldn't have a prayer. Vivian leaned against the back wall, Aldo by her side. She whispered something in his ear and he smiled. The more Tom looked at Aldo, the more he thought the kid was in the wrong business. What other business Aldo could be in was unclear. Maybe he could make himself useful at the Williams Garage. As a human car lift.

Tom ordered a whiskey from the bartender and

watched Mark's performance. Despite what he said about being a numbers guy, the young man knew his way around customers.

"I hoped you would show up tonight."

He caught a whiff of her perfume before he heard her voice. Billie sounded tipsy. She bumped into him with her entire body, a little too hard to be playful. She was off balance.

"What happened to the black suits?" Tom said. "The only one in range is the kid over there and he doesn't look very threatening."

"They're busy setting up the upstairs suite for the party." Billie snickered.

"Party?"

She waved her hands up in the air and shook her hips in a makeshift dance. She lost her footing and Tom caught her. She leaned into him. She was warm and soft. "Big finale. Everybody will be blind drunk within the hour."

"It looks like you're getting a head start."

She pressed her body harder against his. "Yeah, but I'm Sam's property." She laughed. "No party for me. What are you doing later? I'm free. Sort of."

Tom flashed a look at Vivian who was rolling her eyes, irritated at Billie's display of affection. It made him smile. "I shouldn't take liberties with Sam's property."

She put both hands on his chest. "Kiss me." She tilted her head back and grabbed his waist. And froze. In close quarters, the big Colt in the shoulder holster was hard to miss.

Tom didn't give her time to make a sound. He pulled her close and kissed her. To observers, the move looked passionate. When they separated, he propelled her to the entrance of the bar. "You could use some fresh air, Billie."

She was too surprised to resist, and he kept her moving. The grip was standard police technique. It didn't matter that she wore heels, she barely touched the ground. When he released her, they were in the front garden of the hotel and Billie was boiling mad.

"I thought you were a regular joe. A civilian. I must be

cursed, you're a gunslinger like the others."

Tom kept a firm hand on her. It wouldn't do to let her run back in, screaming. "Not really."

"You're a cop?"

He wanted to trust Billie, but it was too much of a risk. "Security for the Avon meeting. My boss got a tad nervous when he learned who shared the building with the delegates." He winked. "He must not have been too worried, or he would have sent the cavalry instead of a lone scout."

Billie chuckled. "And all I wanted was a sexy play with a square. Call me lucky. What are you carrying?"

"I'm used to the Colt. I'm sure your friends go for fancy, stubby, compact artillery. I'm old school."

She pointed at a bench. "You got something against sitting down and taking a breather?"

They looked at the darkening sky and the tapestry of lights from the hotel. Tom had plenty to say but kept quiet. It nagged at him that this smart, funny woman was Sam Giancana's companion. Billie's thoughts were going the same way.

She said: "You like us girls, don't you? I saw you looking at Queenie, Abati's rental."

Tom shook his head. "That's not how I see her. She's a warrior." He took out his cigarettes, lit one. "An Amazon."

Billie laughed, a deep warm laughter that would put impure thoughts in a monk's mind. "What about Jasmine, the Creole girl?"

"Ah, that one … She has X-ray eyes. She can undress a man to the bone." He took a deep drag on his smoke.

"Any insights into the rest of the pack?"

"Probably lost, probably liking the money. Probably scared it won't last as long as they wish it would." He looked at her. "All things that don't apply to you."

"Oh, I'm tainted, all right. Sam is tired of me. He bought a younger model. He can't keep his hands off the kid. I've been putting money away. When I get a chance, I'll pack my things and disappear. Find someplace lazy and warm.

Away from the big cities. There must be a few places like that, forgotten. Where I can sleep all day if I want to. Like a cat. Of course, I might get bored. Do you think I'd make a good Avon lady?"

Tom dug into his jacket pocket and extracted a piece of paper. "You'd take the company by storm. This is June Cavendish's card. She's pure at heart."

"That's intimidating. I'd rather have your card." She took June's anyway and stuck it in her purse. "I don't even know your name."

"Tom."

"Plain and corn-fed. I have a talent. I can tell if a man is good or bad, by touch alone."

"You're going to run a finger down my nose?"

"You'll run your hands down my body."

Tom laughed. "Where did you learn that pick-up line, in some New Orleans house of ill repute?"

"Scared, are you?"

He sighed. She felt wonderful, and once his hands started moving all over her, it was like a dance, the kind that would get them arrested for lewd behavior.

"You're not a security guard," Billie said. "They don't have good hands. Believe me, I know. You have wonderful hands." She pulled away. "I've cooled off now, let's go back."

Tom helped her up, and she slipped her arm into his. Very proper.

"A good man can look evil in the face and remain whole," Billie said.

"What about a good woman?"

"Same." She patted his arm. "But you know that. Goodnight, Tom. Goodbye too. Sam's leaving tomorrow. I might not see you again." She landed a lingering kiss on the corner of his mouth and walked to the elevator. She was straight as a spearhead.

Tom gave a last peek at the bar. The lights were low and the bartender was alone in there, wiping off the counter with a fluffy towel.

He decided against a nightcap. He had the beginning of a headache.

17. Tuesday, May 6

Abati smacked her on the rear.

"You're a professional, Queenie. The *Lieutenants' Ball* is a regular function during a conference. Girls are brought in. The right-hand boys need to have some fun, too. *Fare il tuo dovere.*"

It sounded better in Italian, but she wasn't having any of it. "No way."

He raised an imperious finger. "Get up. Sniff some white stuff and get your ass to the suite on the fourth floor."

"I'm not a coke hound, Mike." She stood with her fists on her hips, furious. "Are all the girls supposed to perform up there?"

"Some are. Not the regulars." He said it as if he was stating the obvious.

"You mean Vicki, Jasmine, Billie, and the rest of the official molls are not forced to go?"

He shook his head. Vivian detected a sheepishness in his expression.

"I have to go because I'm a hooker, is that it?" No answer. "Can't you tell whoever's setting this up that you want to keep me to yourself?" He turned his wide back on her. "Ah, I see. You're afraid to tell them to go to hell. Big Mike Abati is not big enough to raise his voice. Some boss you are!"

He swung around, his arm lifted to slap her. She didn't move an inch, stared at him, boiling inside. He lowered his arm, sighed. "I follow orders, Queenie. You're not part of the inner circle. I don't have a choice. This is how things roll. Leo will look after you. He'll make sure you don't get hurt."

Leo. Loathsome prospect. "Meaning what? He'll rape me first to make sure nobody gets in there before he does?"

"Shut your mouth. Leo won't let anybody beat you up. Or do anything unnatural. Don't ask me to go into details."

"Yeah, it's embarrassing enough. Jesus. Can't Aldo take care of me?"

"He's a kid. This isn't for him. And he's not exactly

lieutenant material."

"Fine," said Vivian, a sharpness in her voice.

"Don't go cold on me, Queenie." He was almost pleading.

Vivian reattached her heels and touched up her face. She avoided looking at Abati; she wanted to punch him.

Leo was outside the room when she stepped into the hallway. He wore a sick leer on his ugly face.

"If you come anywhere near me tonight, you'll end up choking on your balls. Get it?"

"Sure. With all the lambs in the pen, you ain't nuttin' but mutton in my eyes."

"Thank you."

The end of the fourth floor of the hotel was occupied by what looked like a large two-story apartment. A horseshoe-shaped staircase led to a mezzanine that gave access to four bedrooms. The place was in an overheated state. The carousing was well underway when Vivian and Leo walked in. Twenty thugs bustled around a gaggle of girls. Squeezes and strokes were exchanged on divans. The lights were low.

A portable turntable spun bop jazz music to keep people's spirits red hot and groovin' high, and a rolling bar had been set up under a pair of wall sconces, the only bright light in the room. It was manned by a tall fellow, skinny as a fence rail, with blond hair brushed back over the top of his ears in a feminine way. Vivian's eyes lingered on him. He was kept busy pouring out whiskey in tumblers and bubbling champagne in brittle glasses. A girl's scream drew Vivian's attention to a cluster of men seated around a brunette. The girl shrieked with laughter. Two couples were dancing. If that could be called dancing.

Vivian figured she'd better not drink. She found a divan some distance from the testosterone-drunk lieutenants. She pretended to be unconscious and lay back on the soft fabric, the top of her head against a drape-covered wall.

Vivian had been passed around at parties before, but this was worse than any Hollywood affair she'd been hired to attend in the late 30s. Movie men were at least genteel and handsome. The goons in this room were voracious, bold, and ugly. Through half-open eyes, she watched Leo pull a passing blonde down beside him. The woman wrestled with his belt, then his trousers, her head soon moving up and down at his waist. Vivian saw Muriel being dragged up the stairs by a laughing thug, while another one followed behind feeling under her dress with his killer's hands. Muriel wasn't exempt from these shenanigans; Joe Piranio wanted to punish her, obviously. The girl was expendable. He would discard her. The message was clear.

Vivian's glare held off an eager guy, but her intimidation tactics wouldn't work for long. The temperature was rising in the room, and the plays grew rawer.

Two men moved her way. She played dead.

"Is this Abati's girl?"

Two sets of leather shoes scraped to a stop beside her lounger. She made snoring sounds.

"Calling her a girl might be stretching it. Look at the sag in those tits. She's a looker, for sure, but she must be forty."

A weighty man sat on either side of her. Her head lolled as they joggled her torso between them. One of the men poured a glass of champagne onto her face. Vivian coughed and sputtered when liquid went down her nose.

"Hey, Mommy. Wake up." One of the men pinched her nose between his fingers. "I need you to suck my cock."

The other man laughed.

"Did you get a look at that short-haired blonde 'Mooney Sam' brought with him? Wow. She might be eighteen, but I doubt it. I bet she's tight. Like a kid glove."

"Kid is right." The man chuckled. "Sam's making Billie sleep in her own room. Can you believe it? Why did he even bring her? She should be here tonight. I've been wanting to plow her since the convention in New Orleans in forty-eight. I should go down to two-o-five. I bet I could charm that big blonde bitch right onto her back." He yawned. "Jesus, I'm tired. Giancana's not gonna need Billie for long after he gets home. I might as well inherit her, right?"

"He ain't gettin' home. It's happening right here. Not on his territory. On ours."

Vivian began to snore again. *Keep talking, you idiots.*

"Who's doing it?"

"Some pro from out of town."

"You know him?"

"Nope. No idea who it is. It's a done deal, according to the boss. I bet it's gonna happen at the rodeo tomorrow. Maybe in the crowd. With a blade."

"Are you kidding me?"

"How would you do it?"

"I'd plug him from a distance. High-powered rifle. Nobody would see me. Clean getaway."

"He'd be hard to plug in a crowd. And what if he gets a tummy ache and stays home? He hasn't gone to town with us once. Trafficante didn't go either. Chances are they won't make the trek to the rodeo. It'd be better to hit him here. At the meeting. Get right in his face and let him know the score before you rub him out."

"Then what?"

"The stockyard operations are gonna move down to Missouri where they belong." The man's hands roamed between Vivian's legs. "Then there's his liquor and numbers operations."

Vivian felt her skirt being lifted. Her mind whirred behind the pretend snores. Giancana. He was the target? She opened her eyes just enough to recognize the men. They belonged to Anthony Gizzo, the Kansas City boss. His lieutenants talked too much. Gizzo should blow their empty brains.

She had to find Tom.

"I'm gonna be sick." She struggled to sit up.

"Shut up. We don't believe you. Nothing makes you broads sick." The man pulled her off the couch. "We gonna find ourselves a nice cozy room up that nifty staircase and have some fun."

"I'll go grab us a bottle or two," the other man said.

Vivian was being pushed by a hard hand toward the staircase.

"Your boss, Abati, is a chump. He's got no standing out here. Neither do you. You're small time. The both of you."

Vivian swallowed her rage. He was right. She'd never felt so small.

18. Wednesday, May 7

The banging on the door screamed of an emergency.

Tom had just fixed a drink from the room's well-appointed bar. It was late, well past midnight, but he was too tense to sleep. Vivian occupied his mind. Too many unknowns. What if she was dragged to the rodeo tomorrow? What if Muriel refused to hit the road with them or made a scene? He didn't care if the girl came, but Vivian had adopted her and would make a fuss if the redhead held back. What if the thugs all decided to take a dip in the pool just as he and the girls were about to make their exit? He could handle Aldo. He couldn't fight an army.

The banging on the door didn't let up.

He opened, half expecting to see June Cavendish or Billie. It was Vivian and she looked ragged, make-up running, clothes askew. He'd never seen her like that. She was always so put together, so much in control.

"Look at me. If you can stand it." She was shivering.

Tom grabbed her clammy upper arm and pulled her inside. "Are you hurt? What happened?" She jerked her arm out of his grip.

"I'm a whore. And it shows." The words came like bursts of spit. "It shouldn't bother me anymore, but I can take only so much."

He closed the door and ran a hand over her back. He meant it to be soothing. It reminded him of his mother and childhood woes.

"If you touch me again, I'll punch your face in."

"I'm sorry." He stepped back. "Who did this to you?"

"I wish I could remember them all. Tonight's the night when the top lieutenants get to fuck their little hearts out. A holiday tradition. A special treat for the loyal boys." She reached for him. "You can hold me now." She wrapped her arms around him and placed her head on his shoulder. Her hair smelled of smoke, alcohol, and sweat.

"You're here," Tom muttered. "There's no reason to

wait. We can leave right now. We'll be miles away before anybody realizes you're gone."

"Shut up. Hold me."

The stink in her hair was getting to him.

Vivian's voice was low. "When you came to Pepper's the first time, Otis warned me about you. He said you had these gray eyes that could turn to ice in an instant. It's bullshit. Your eyes are always kind. The thugs I'm running with have eyes of stone."

She talked with her mouth in his shirt, in the hollow of his shoulder. He felt the warmth of her breath. She had stopped shivering and gone limp. He adjusted his hold on her, concerned she might slide to the floor.

She raised her head. "They are not human, Tom."

"Unfortunately, they are." He broke their embrace. "Let's get you cleaned up."

He half carried her to the bathroom, sat her on the side of the tub, and opened the faucet. She didn't seem injured, but she was punched out, drained of her strength. He removed her shoes and pulled her up. She swayed and held on to him.

"I'm sorry," she muttered.

He unzipped her dress and she stepped out of it. She seemed unsure her legs would support her.

The only light in the bathroom was a fluorescent tube on top of the medicine cabinet over the sink but it was enough to show an array of stains on the silk of her dress. Not blood. At least the bastards hadn't gone that far. There were angry bruises on her arms, and around her neck, on her collarbone. Tom felt the anger building up.

"I've had so many men." Her voice seemed to come from a distance. "So many I didn't choose. It was my job when I was a kid. My choice to do the job. I had the looks and the guts. I got by. I've been passed around. But not like tonight. Never like tonight. With so much hate. So much ... contempt. Tom?"

He kneeled in front of her to work on her stocking clips. "Yes."

"Look at me."

He raised his head. There were tears in her eyes.

"You don't have to say anything, Viv."

"I want to. Listen. It's important. Until tonight, the men who took me, they all wanted something I had, something that was *mine, me*. I didn't always want to give it to them, but that's irrelevant." She pointed a finger at her chest, poked at it. "It was still *me*. The stone eyes tonight, they looked and I was nothing." She shook her head. "Not even a lousy *thing*. Do you understand?"

He nodded and put both hands on her thighs, on the black silk straps and the little metal clasps that held up her nylons.

"Don't let them off the hook, Vivian. Others make that mistake and call these kinds of people monsters. I know better and so do you. They *are* human, and it is terrifying what humans can do. You have to look at it straight and not flinch."

He remembered what Billie said, in the garden. *A good man can look evil in the face and remain whole*. She added it was the same for a woman. Vivian was broken right now, her soul quivering in the dark. He had to coax it back to the light. And be gentle, extremely.

He worked the clips and rolled down her stockings. She had bruises there too, on the inside and outside of her thighs, the cruel marks of hard digging fingers.

"You have good hands," she whispered, unknowingly echoing Billie's words. "Do you do this for Rachel?"

"It gives her a thrill."

"I bet."

He stood up and checked the water in the tub. "You can handle the rest, get in there."

She took off her bra, garter belt, and panties, delicate black lace things that showed traces of ripping.

"I'm getting old, Tommy. I should get respectable someday." She eased into the large bathtub.

"I can't imagine you respectable. Now dunk. Get under."

"What?"

"I'm going to wash that sticky stuff out of your hair."

Tom put a hand on her head and pushed down, not too hard, he didn't want to scare her. She was feeling better already, he could see it, but her nerves were frayed. He sat on the side of the tub and grabbed the shampoo, got a good lather going. She hummed something from a bebop melody while his fingers ran through her dark tresses.

"Damn, you're good," she said. "I feel this all the way down my spine. Are you having the boner of the century?"

"What do you think?"

"I think that's cute, Detective. And it may surprise you, but I don't even want to see it."

"I understand."

"Maybe I've had enough of that thing for one lifetime."

He lifted the sprayer from its tray over the faucet, moved the diverter, and opened the hot water valve. He held the sprayer over her soapy head. He wasn't surprised to see a few gray hairs. "Lean forward." He rinsed until she relaxed under the hot spray. "Washing your hair is one thing, but I might lose control if I touch any more of you. I'll make you a drink."

He left the bathroom before the steam made him dizzy. It was more than the steam.

*

Vivian found a robe hanging on the door and used Tom's comb to untangle her hair. She left a few dark strands in the teeth as a souvenir. The underwear was ruined, but she'd have to slip the soiled garments back onto her clean body. Maybe she shouldn't have stopped at Tom's on the way to Mike Abati's room. What would her boss think if his whore came home smelling like a rose? Unless being on his own, without her to entertain him, he drank himself silly and was fast asleep.

She had a brief thought of Tom in bed, waiting for her, and shook it away.

He was in an armchair with his long legs stretched on the coffee table. He pointed at the sofa, at a dewy glass on a side table.

"I made it strong," he said.

"You should open a practice. Specialty: bruised and winged whores. You have a generous bedside manner. I could get used to that. In another life."

He smiled. "You're yourself again. I was serious about leaving immediately. You've shaken off your escort, and after what they've been doing at the party none of these guys will be able to shoot straight."

"Don't bundle Aldo with the rest. He wasn't invited." She gathered the robe around her and settled onto the sofa with a grimace. Her hip hurt. An old injury. The recent contortions didn't help. "The situation has changed. I have new information."

He sighed. "God, not again. You're a regular Mata Hari."

"I hope not. Her career didn't end well."

"I don't think she was very bright. There's nothing at stake anymore, Viv. The feds are gone. We've been cut loose. We don't owe anything to anybody. I wish we'd left yesterday. I passed your Mexican Brown information to Pete Delgado. He was very interested. Maybe the FBI will do something with it, but I doubt it. They have a talent for missing the mark."

She took a sip of the whiskey. The heat felt good but the pounding in her head returned and she leaned on the back of the sofa with her eyes closed. "I overheard something while two creeps were doing me over."

"Stop. I don't want details. I might kill somebody."

"Over me? That's so sweet of you. You want to know or not?"

He took a deep breath. "All right, you'll tell anyway. What have you got?"

"I know who the Eraser's target is."

"Don't tell me Sinatra is back on the record player." He hummed "That Old Black Magic".

"If he was, I wouldn't bother to tell you. A couple of Gizzo's boys thought I was passed out. They'd had a lot to drink and talked about a hit on Sam Giancana." She took another sip of the booze. "They didn't know where or when, but it's gonna happen here, in Kansas, on Gizzo's turf."

"Has to be tomorrow. Today, rather. Sam's leaving."

"How do you know?"

"Billie told me."

Vivian pulled her legs under her. "That narrows down the possibilities. Giancana won't go to the rodeo. He hasn't gone to town yet and he won't do it on the day he leaves. The Eraser will either take a shot in the hotel or plug him when he comes out the door. Both options are tricky. The hotel is a snakes' nest. If Gomma tries to nail Sam between the hotel and his car, it won't be an easy shot. He's always surrounded by bodyguards. The Eraser is good, but he might never have an opening. Or he could be lying in wait on the road. Wreck the car and finish off whoever's still standing. That's the way I'd do it."

Tom lit a cigarette and sank deeper in the armchair. "The feds told me that Giancana and Trafficante travel in a four-car convoy. A lone assassin can't attack a motorcade. It has to be an ambush in the hotel. Bystanders might get hurt. You're sure Gomma has the contract?"

"Gizzo's thugs said the killer was an out-of-towner. Who else could it be?" She sat up, suddenly, eyes wide. "Damn it, I saw him!"

"Where?"

"In the suite, at the party. He was the bartender. In a sick yellow wig. Jesus, I could have grabbed a gun from any of those pigs and finished him."

Tom stared at the bottom of his glass. "He's here already. That changes everything."

She shrugged. "When people start running, nobody will give a shit about us. Where's your car?"

"We can't let it happen, Viv. Giancana is the man on the rise. His death will start a gang war. People will die, innocents among them. Machine guns aren't selective. When the feds left, I went to the KC police. The troopers stationed around The Elms know about Gomma; they have his description. I hoped they would catch him, but he sneaked through. We can't have cops search the hotel, not with dozens of armed maniacs in residence."

She sniggered. "Let it ride."

"I can't do that. We have to warn Giancana. Get him out of here. I'll talk to Billie. She's close to him."

"Not so much anymore and I doubt she gives a damn. Sam has a new young thing in his bed. Billie wants out. I told you I saw her with Gizzo. What do you think they were talking about? I also saw her slip something to Gizzo's driver. Billie is in this up to her neck."

Tom shook his head. "She wouldn't be involved in a murder."

"And you know that how?"

"She doesn't have a mean bone in her body. Gizzo is using her. You have to get Mike Abati on board."

"You're out of your mind. I can't do that!"

Tom leaned forward in his chair. "Think about it. Giancana is set to rule the roost. He's got the brains and the ambition. Imagine what Abati could win from a close association with the man. Abati isn't friends with Gizzo, is he?"

Vivian recalled what the two men said before they raped her. *Abati is a chump. You're small time*. "Gizzo despises Mike."

"You think Abati is smart enough to set a trap for the killer?"

She made a face. "No way. He'll go straight for Gizzo's throat, and that'll start a gang war there and then."

"Cooler heads must prevail. Giancana's hopefully. Can you take me to Billie's room?"

"No." She raised a hand. "It has nothing to do with you two being chummy. The second floor is guarded. You're an outsider, you won't get through. I'll send Billie to you." She stood and walked to the bathroom. "I'll put my rags back on."

"Don't send Billie. Come with her."

"Minor detail, how do I explain our relationship?"

"Billie thinks I'm working security for the Avon conference. You couldn't go to the cops with your discovery. You came to me."

"We're lucky she fancies you, she'll believe anything you say."

*

Vivian walked back to her room and changed clothes. Abati snored loud enough to make the windowpanes rattle. He wouldn't be asking for her any time soon. She cursed softly. She should have jumped on Tom's suggestion to leave right away, but no, she had to impress him. *Look at me, Mr. Detective darling, see what I found out!* Just her luck to be working with a damn principled cop ... now she was saddled with saving a mobster's life. A man she didn't give a fig about. A man who might be responsible for sending her to that rotten party.

She searched Abati's belongings for a weapon but there wasn't one. What kind of Mob boss was he? It was irritating. She was tired of being toothless.

The goon who fantasized about screwing Billie said she was in room 205.

As Vivian came out of the room, Aldo appeared around the hallway corner. His eyes lit up when he spotted his wayward lamb.

She didn't give him time to ask questions. "Where have you been? I've looked for you in every cranny of this damned hotel. I feel naked without you by my side."

"I was looking for you, too, Queenie. I can't find anybody. The bar is empty."

"It's late, kid. Maybe they all went to bed."

"Where's Leo?"

"Last time I saw him, he was in a suite on the fourth floor." She hoped he was still in there, stone drunk and fucked empty. If he found her roaming the corridors at night with Aldo, there would be hell to pay. "Come with me. You're armed, right?"

He patted his armpit. "Where are we going?"

"To get Billie. Don't ask why."

There were no guards outside room 205. A couple of them stood watch in front of suite 200, Giancana's. The men gave Vivian and Aldo a hard look, ready hands hovering near their holstered guns. She turned her back on them and knocked on Billie's door. There was no answer. She tried the handle. The room was unlocked. She poked the light switch.

It was almost two a.m., according to her wristwatch, and Billie's bed hadn't been slept in. Clothes lay on the end of the bed, next to an empty box with a picture of a bathing suit on the lid.

Vivian led Aldo to the spa area. The pool steamed in darkness, an eerie sight, misty, with the safety lights glowing around the edges like keen animal eyes in a swamp. Vivian walked around. Aldo's leather shoes clacked on the tile. Too loud.

"Can you muffle the clippety-clop? You sound like Ann Miller in *Easter Parade*."

"Sorry." He pointed at a cluster of chairs. "I think there's somebody over there."

The pool lights put green highlights on a blond head. Billie. She was wrapped in a white robe.

"Is she all right?" Aldo said.

"She's asleep." Vivian grabbed the woman by a shoulder and shook her. "Wake up."

Billie opened her eyes. "Queenie? What the ..." She saw Aldo's hulking shape behind Vivian. "If you've come to drag me to that fucking party, you'll have to knock me out first." She pulled her legs under her and yawned. "It's warm here. I like warm. Have you ever been to Phoenix?"

"Not that I remember. Get up, Billie, we have to go. Something happened."

"I don't have to go anywhere. Not anymore. Sam has a new toy. He brought me along on this damn trip to show the whole gaggle of them that I don't matter anymore. Well, fuck him, I claim my freedom. Right here and now."

"Fine sentiment but we need you."

"Nobody needs broads like us. You should know that

by now."

Vivian was about to ask Aldo to sling Billie over his shoulder to get the show moving, when she saw another body stretched out on a nearby lounger. "Is that Muriel? She was at the party."

"She stumbled in here about an hour ago and fell right in the pool. I pulled her out before she drowned. Dropped her on the chair and she went right to sleep. Piranio beats her up and then makes her perform at the big whoop-de-do. Talk about being slapped around."

"Aldo, you stay here and keep an eye on Muriel. Billie, we gotta move." This was taking too long. Tom must be itching to go to Giancana by now.

Aldo pulled a lounger next to Muriel and sat on the edge of it with his elbows on his knees, focused on the girl. She was in good hands.

Billie took in the scene, frowning. She sat up. "He works for you now? What's going on?"

"I overheard two mugs at the party, Gizzo's boys. I pretended to be asleep and they kept shooting their mouths off about a hit on your boss. A professional's been hired for the job."

"Tough luck. Sam leaves in the morning."

"I know. The killer must know too. We have to hustle. Get your ass out of the chair, Billie."

"You're with Abati. Why do you care what happens to some boss with more testosterone than all his lieutenants put together? Call a cab and get yourself out of here before the shooting starts." She pointed at Aldo who was staring at Muriel with his big brown sheepdog eyes. "Haul these two with you while you're at it. Babes in the woods." She shivered despite the heat. "This ain't a place for innocents."

"If there's gunplay in the hotel, innocents will get hurt."

"Not much we can do, Queenie." She sniggered. "You want to call the cops?"

"That'll add gasoline to the fire. I didn't know where to

go with the information. I told everything to that guy from Avon. The hunk you've been flirting with. I thought he might round up all these women and their lipsticks and get them out of here."

Billie grinned. "You knew where to find him? That's handy, Queenie. I saw how you looked at him. I bet he ran his hands and his big gun all over you, too. Damn it, I'm really stupid. Falling for that baggage." She looked away.

Vivian shook her head. "I'd just left the party. The shape I was in, he had no interest in fucking me."

"Taking up with men outside the family is a sure way to get killed. Leave, honey. The game will play out no matter what. With our luck, he's probably a fed."

"I don't know what he is. All I know is that he told me to find you."

And now I've found you and let's get moving.

"Jesus Christ, for a whore, you're pathetic." Billie swung her legs off the lounger and cinched her robe. "All right. Let's go. Think he can handle both of us? It's been a while since I had a threesome."

Vivian sighed. "We're going to go talk to the boss, Aldo." Let him believe she meant Mike Abati. "Stay here and make sure Muriel is safe. Billie says a guy is after her."

"Sure thing, Queenie."

Vivian patted his shoulder. "Wait right here for me."

*

Vivian's knock on the door sounded less urgent this time. Tom noticed she'd changed her clothes. Billie looked like she'd spent the night at the Turkish baths.

"Either Billie comes to get you," Tom said, "or Abati will have to go talk to Giancana."

"Not my favorite option." Vivian pushed Billie inside and pulled the door closed.

"Hey, where you going?" Billie said.

"She'll wake up Mike Abati." Tom pointed at the spot on the sofa where Vivian had nestled earlier. "Please sit down." He took the armchair again.

"What are you up to? What's this about a hit on Sam?"

"Gizzo is staging a coup. The man he hired is in the hotel, hiding somewhere. There's no time to search the place. You have to wake Giancana, and he needs to leave. Now. It makes no sense for him to make a stand, Billie. There's no telling who'll fall when the bullets start flying."

"I'm out of favor, buddy. What do I care if Sam gets plugged?"

"You want out, right? You don't think Giancana will reward you for saving his life? You want to be the first one to tell him about the hit. Don't let Abati beat you to it."

"What do you care? Who are you? A fucking fed? You've got Queenie wrapped around your finger, and you want to do the same to me."

Tom chuckled. "The FBI's clueless, sweetie. Mr. Hoover doesn't believe organized crime exists. He could come here, spend the week, and return home convinced he attended a meatpacking conference. The man is blind as a mole."

"You don't look like a local cop. Too smooth. Too well-spoken."

"You want me to caress you again, Billie, to confirm I'm one of the good guys? I'd love to but we don't have the time."

"Maybe it's a trap, what about that? I help you get Sam out of his room, and he meets a bullet in the hallway, or by the exit door. Smart play."

She had a point. And they were wasting time haggling. Tom hated putting the screws on her. "I'm not the one who had lunch with Gizzo, Billie."

She jumped to her feet. "Fuck you!" Her eyes went to the side table, to the Colt in the holster.

Tom only had to reach to beat her to the gun. He grabbed her one-handed and she fell on him. The armchair creaked. He held her tight, in his lap.

"Fun tumble. In different circumstances I would enjoy it. Warn Giancana. Don't let Abati take all the credit. You can use this. You can be free. Nobody needs to know what you were cooking with Gizzo. Queenie won't say a word, and I won't either. Use your brain, honey."

"Tell me the truth, who are you?"

He sighed. "I'm a detective with the San Francisco Police Department. I was sent here to keep an eye on Mike Abati. He's a big player in my hometown. If he comes back with juicy deals, I want to know. Satisfied?"

She looked him straight in the eye. He held her gaze.

"Kiss me," she said.

"Another test of my goodness at heart?"

"Oh, shut up."

He released his grip enough for her to lean in. It was a very nice kiss that did something to the back of his neck, little nerves in there that enjoyed a tingle.

She slipped off his lap. "If you faked that kiss, you're the best liar on the planet. I'll wake up Sam."

Tom slipped on the holster, put on his jacket and hat.

"You're coming with me?" Billie said.

"And be used for target practice? I'll walk down the stairs with you. You do your job, and I'll do mine."

*

Tom waited on the second-floor landing until he heard a murmur of voices. He peeked into the hallway. Billie was talking to two bodyguards. Giancana's muscle. They patted her down—not much she could hide under that bathrobe—and opened the door of the suite for her.

Tom had no doubt she would convince Giancana. The man lived under the gun.

Apart from the two goons on the second floor, Tom didn't see anybody. Gomma had chosen the perfect window for the hit. After the party, the Mob soldiers wouldn't be in fighting mode for a while. Murder Inc. would sleep late.

The ground floor of the hotel was deserted and the bar was dark. A uniformed employee, black crewcut and a nose like a cattle chute—Detective Campbell's description was accurate—sat behind the reception desk, reading. He looked up as Tom approached, raised from his chair, and closed his book, leaving a finger in to mark the page.

"Can I help you, sir?"

Tom reached in his breast pocket and the man tensed. He was very much awake and aware. The finger came out of the book. John Ross Macdonald's *The Drowning Pool*. Good book. Tom had read it.

"You're Eric Robinson. Detective Campbell told me about you." Tom put his badge on the counter. "Tom Keegan, Homicide, San Francisco PD."

The fake concierge relaxed. "Campbell said you were here."

"Gomma was spotted in a suite upstairs, tending bar at a Mob party."

Robinson let out a curse. "How did he get in?"

"Doesn't matter. I need your help, Robinson."

"I'll call it in. We'll search the place."

"And wake up the Mafia brigade?"

Robinson grunted. "It could get sticky."

"It's in everybody's interest to keep things quiet. I know who Gomma's target is. The man is being warned as we speak. He'll leave soon."

"Remove the mark, remove the hit." Robinson nodded. "What do you want me to do?"

"KC police have a perimeter in place. I need to talk to whoever's in charge on the main access road. The escape car will come barreling down."

"A good reason for troopers to shoot. Who's the target?"

Tom hesitated. "I can't tell you."

"I understand. Sheriff Mayer is the man to see. There's one road out of here. It connects with the main avenue, Kansas City to the south-west, Saint Louis to the east. Mayer is near the intersection. There are ways around but I doubt people in a hurry will meander down goat tracks."

"I know the intersection. I've driven in and out of here a couple of times," Tom said.

"I'll call dispatch and let Mayer know you're coming.

That it?"

"Is there a way to isolate the east wing?"

"The hallways run through." Robinson frowned. "I see what you're getting at. You want to separate the civilians from the gunslingers."

"Everybody's fast asleep right now, but if there's a disturbance ..."

"I have four officers scattered around. I could put them on the connecting landings, between the wings, but they'll be in the direct line of fire if the hitman comes running with mobsters on his tail. I'm not eager to put our guys in that position. I'd rather use them to go knock on doors and tell people to remain inside. If we had time, I'd put them in fireman's gear and make up a training exercise of some kind."

Tom thought the idea had merit. "We have an hour, maybe two, not more than that. Gomma has to act while the goons are still reeling from the party and the rest of the guests are asleep. Let's bring in a few fire trucks, ambulances, and cop cars. It might do the trick and keep chaos to a minimum. Nobody shoots firefighters and medics." He didn't add that if guns were fired, they would have a leg up on the emergency.

"I'll give the calls. What about arresting Gomma?" Robinson said.

"If he slips away, I'm all right with him eating a bullet somewhere else. Thanks, Eric."

"Pleasure, Tom."

He turned away from the desk and stopped. "No sirens, just the lights. And tell the convoy lead to stop at Sheriff Mayer's checkpoint for a quick briefing."

Robinson gave him a thumbs up. He was already dialing.

Tom ran through the spa, the shortest way to the back, and sprinted along the swimming pool. The moist hot air was stifling. He hit the access to the outdoor pool at full speed. Another dash along the rippling water and he reached the door he planned to use for their escape. Locked. Of course. Events had caught him wrong footed. He climbed the fence. He would deal with the locked door on the way back.

He had to find Sheriff Mayer before the lawman did Gomma's job for him.

19. Wednesday, May 7

Vivian shook Mike Abati out of his deep torpor. She had to put a pillow over his face to get him to sputter into alertness. He had excuses, it was the darkest time of night.

"Mike, darling, we need to go to Giancana's room. Now."

"Momo?" he blurted. "What about?"

"You're taking me to him. I have information that could save his life. You're my boss. It's time to make an impression. Get dressed. Quick. Billie will be here soon."

"Billie? Information? What information?" His eyes were unfocused. He was working hard to understand the words she was throwing at him and not making much progress.

"You'll hear it when Sam hears it. We don't have time to go over all that again."

"If it's a joke, I swear I'll beat the skin off your ass, Queenie."

"You can have my ass on a plate. It's not a joke."

When the knock on the door came, Abati's eyes went big as golf balls.

"I'll be damned," he muttered.

Billie stood in the opening, still in her bathrobe. "You're dressed, good. Sam's waiting."

The hallways were dark and silent. The bodyguards usually posted near the elevators and at both ends of the corridors were nowhere to be seen. Did Gizzo buy them off or were they still upstairs, marinating in sex and booze?

Giancana's suite had the same two tough guys as before planted in front. They searched Abati and Vivian for weapons before Billie led them in.

In the central room of the suite, Giancana sat behind a desk and Sonny Trafficante was ensconced in an armchair. The lights were low and the curtains pulled close. Vivian nodded in approval. They knew how to avoid being easy targets.

"Tell me what you heard," Giancana said. "The exact

words."

Vivian wasn't easily intimidated. She'd put bullets in the heads of powerful men. There was something about Sam and Sonny that put them in a category apart. They weren't particularly attractive, but they were shrewd. Violent, sure, but cold-blooded and calculating. Crime was their business, a power machine.

She told the story with measured words, no add-ons, no commentary. These men didn't care what happened to her, and frankly the entire episode was starting to fade from her memory. Tom unrolling her stockings left a much stronger impression.

"This better be on the level, Queenie," Abati growled.

"Shut up." Trafficante steepled his hands, thoughtful. "How do you know for sure they were Gizzo's men?"

"I've seen them with him, at the cattle show. They also said 'here, our territory', that's Kansas City."

"They hired a contract killer."

"Yes, somebody from out of town."

"No names?"

This was the delicate bend in the road. She was a rented girl. What did she know about professional assassins?

"They shot their mouth about the hit but they didn't know the details. One of them said it would be at the rodeo, the other said it was at the hotel. One said stabbing, the other said shooting. They said it was a done deal and all the stockyard business would move to KC." She shook her head. "No names."

"We have to leave right now," Trafficante said.

Vivian repressed a smile. The man thought like Tom. Avoid a confrontation. Get out fast.

Giancana protested. "Like thieves in the night? *Vergogna*!"

Trafficante shrugged impatiently. Vivian agreed with him. This wasn't a time for pride.

"Nobody needs to know." Abati seemed surprised by his own words, but now that he had started he jumped in all the way. "We can get you down the fire escape. Pretend somebody is still in the room, turn on the lights, order breakfast, all that."

"One look and they'll know our cars are gone," Giancana said.

"Take Gizzo's."

Vivian glanced at Abati. Maybe she underestimated the man. He might not be bright, but he was cunning.

"I like it," Trafficante said. "If the hit is planned for here, at the hotel, Gizzo will want to be on site to claim the prize, rally the troops. Hail to the Chief. He won't drive anywhere." He clapped his hands together. "Let's do it. Billie, go pack."

"What about me?"

All eyes turned to the bedroom door. The flapper girl stood there in a sheer nightgown. The light pink fabric stopped below her narrow hips. She leaned against the doorframe, her short haircut highlighted by the freckles on her nose. She was just a kid. Her fingers moved along the wood trim. It was a picture meant to inflame. Vivian felt like slapping the girl. Did she realize what was at stake? The entire scene must fly well over her head.

Giancana wasn't distracted for long. "You pack too, sweetheart. And be quick about it."

The girl smirked at Billie and disappeared into the bedroom.

"You know Gizzo's ride, Mike?" Giancana said.

Abati stood briefly stunned.

"Eldorado," Vivian muttered, looking at Billie. "Missouri plates."

"Cadillac Eldorado. Missouri plates," Abati said.

"Good work." Giancana stood behind the desk. "It's decided. Mike, you and your crew take care of the make-believe. Keep it up until lunch time. Nobody knows about this except the people in this room. We take the two men posted at the door with us. We'll need replacements for them. For appearances."

Trafficante extracted himself from the armchair. "I'll give you two of mine, but my best cover man is coming with us. So is Georgina. My boys will remain outside the door and report to you, Abati, but I want them back after this is all over." He slipped out the door, one hand in his pocket.

"What do you want me to do about Gizzo?" Abati said.

He was on the ball tonight, Vivian was impressed.

"Nothing," Giancana said. "Keep your wits about yourself, Mike. Gizzo is my problem. He'll be dealt with my way. There will be changes. Your loyalty will be rewarded."

Vivian lifted the window sash and looked at the parking lot. A fire escape ran past the bedroom window. She leaned out, half expecting to see Gomma hulking on the steps. She let her eyes adjust to the dimness. Nothing suspicious.

Trafficante returned to the room a few minutes later with his favorite bodyguard. He brought Giancana's muscle in with him. A tough-looking brunette with large breasts glowered at everyone. Her suitcase had been packed so fast something silky dragged on the floor.

"My boys are outside," Trafficante said. "Let's go."

Giancana shook Abati's hand. "I will not forget this." He gave a brief nod to Vivian. "Thank you."

Billie came into the suite carrying her suitcase. The blond baby doll had just emerged from the bedroom with hers. The room was crowded.

"Billie should stay here, at The Elms," Vivian said.

"What are you talking about? My girls ride with me. Always."

"One girl should be enough for the trip. You won't have room in that car for eight. Besides, Billie is known to everyone here. She's Giancana's best girl. Billie's the one people remember. She should be seen having breakfast in the café. No one would believe you left her behind." No one would believe she handed an envelope to Gizzo's driver, either.

"I won't leave without her," Giancana said.

"It's better if I stay, Sam. Keep the girl safe. She's just a kid."

Where Billie found that motherly tone, Vivian had no idea. It was quite a performance.

The little flapper snorted in disgust. Vivian rolled her eyes. Snooty and spoiled. Guaranteed to get on Giancana's nerves before long.

Trafficante handed a couple of room keys to Abati. "You and your dark-haired firecracker should spend the night here. Would look weird if you showed up in the morning jangling the keys."

"Mike. Hit the lights, please." Vivian pushed the window sash as high as it would go. She detached the screen and set it aside.

Giancana's men squeezed out onto the fire escape landing. Then Georgina and Trafficante with their suitcases, followed by Trafficante's best gun. Last came the flapper and Giancana with their bags. It was the most awkward conga line Vivian had ever witnessed. She hoped the stairs would hold them all. She reattached the screen and watched as the silhouettes moved into the dark shadows of the parking lot. Billie and Abati joined her at the window, breathing quietly until the sound of a V-8 roared to life.

It would be a tight fit, the seven of them, in Gizzo's Cadillac. Vivian guessed they would ditch the car as soon as they could get in touch with associates and find more suitable transportation.

She watched the car drive away with the lights switched off, black on black, thieves in the night indeed. Abati locked himself in the bathroom.

"I'll go back to my room." Billie stopped at the door. "Thanks for the break. In the morning, I'll hang out downstairs, until lunchtime. Then I'm out of here. The palm trees are calling."

"Good luck," Vivian said. "I hope whatever Gizzo paid for that envelope is enough to start your new life."

"I hope so, too."

"Damn it, Queenie." Abati walked out of the bathroom

wiping his face with a handkerchief. "What a show."

Billie closed the door behind her.

"It's not over, Mike. I expect fireworks."

"You think the killer will still try something?"

"He doesn't know Giancana's gone, so yeah, he'll try. Let's go to bed. With two guards outside, we should be safe."

"You're very calm about all this," he said.

"I'm happy they're gone. You're in a dangerous business, Mike."

He winked. "I'm not big enough to be a target, like Giancana and Trafficante."

"You're plenty big for me, babe."

He chuckled. "Look at this place. How much does it go for?" He explored Giancana's suite. It was a lot bigger than his room. "Leo behaved with you, at the party?"

"He didn't bother me. I told him I would kill him."

He watched her undress and slip naked under the covers.

"Better set the alarm, Mike. We can't sleep in."

He fiddled with the clock, then sat on the side of the bed, in silence, for a while. "I don't know who you are, Queenie." He kicked off his shoes and removed his jacket. "If you ever want a job as one of my lieutenants, just say the word."

He turned off the light and undressed in the dark.

20. Wednesday, May 7

They saw the car at the last moment, but they'd heard it coming from some distance away.

"A V-8," Sheriff Mayer said. "Has to be your guys."

One second there was only darkness and a second later two powerful lights came on.

"They're not stupid enough to run blind," Mayer said. "We slink back and do nothing? That's the idea?"

It bothered Tom. What if the hit had happened and it was Gomma in the car, or Gizzo? He needed to be sure.

"Hand me your flashlight."

He stepped off the grassy shoulder onto the road, turned on the flashlight and pointed it at the oncoming car. He flashed it on and off three times.

"You're crazy," Mayer shouted.

"Stay back."

The car, a black hulking shape, slowed down but didn't stop. It inched forward. Tom was fully visible in the powerful beams. He pointed the flashlight at the ground, kept his arms away from his body. The car stopped ten yards away. The purr of the V-8 was ominous in the quiet night. Nocturnal animals had gone to bed and early birds weren't up yet.

Tom walked to the car, driver side. He perceived movement inside, heads. It wasn't Gomma. He would be alone.

The driver rolled his window down. He had one hand on the wheel. Tom could guess what the other one was doing. They were crowded in there. Three men on the front bench. He was careful not to point the flashlight in anybody's eyes, and slanted it just enough to make features, harsh, etched by the stark play of light and shadow.

"What's going on?" the driver said.

Tom ignored him, focusing on the back of the car. Four people. Two men, two women. Giancana and Trafficante. A brunette, not Vivian, and a blonde, not Billie. He breathed easier.

"A dangerous individual has been spotted in the area.

His description has been given to law enforcement agencies. The Clay County Sheriff Department established mobile checkpoints. Thank you for stopping. You can be on your way now. Drive carefully."

Giancana put a hand on the driver's shoulder. He leaned forward. "Does that individual have a name?"

Tom smiled. Nobody was fooled here. "Donato Gomma, aka the Eraser. He has a long record."

"Thank you, Officer, uh, Deputy?"

"Detective. Sir."

"I hope you catch him."

"Unless he retires, a bullet will find him. Eventually."

Giancana nodded. They looked at each other, in silence; they didn't blink. A quiet reckoning. Tom took a step back. Giancana tapped the driver's shoulder, and the car moved slowly forward. Both the driver's hands were on the wheel now.

Tom walked back to the grassy shoulder and Sheriff Mayer.

"You have some stones. Is it who you thought it was?"

"Yeah. One weight off my back. Thanks for the help, Sheriff."

"Nothing will happen now, right?"

"We can't relax. Gomma is a sly customer. He won't come down the main road in a Cadillac."

Tom was tired. It wasn't daybreak yet and he was used to sleepless nights but these moments with Giancana should be counted in dog years. There was something about the man. And Trafficante too, who said nothing, didn't move a muscle during the entire exchange, and managed to exude the kind of menace that stuck in the back of your mind.

He looked down the road, at the fading lights of the Caddy. A flash of red in the opposite direction caught his eye. It was the convoy of fire trucks and ambulances called by Detective Robinson.

"We're going to have help, Sheriff," he said.

Mayer groaned. "I don't trust a firefighter to handle

law enforcement."

"No, but people like them."

They waited for the first engine to reach the patrol car that sat on the shoulder with its lights on.

Bringing the fire department and ambulance crews up to speed on the events at The Elms took a while, with questions. Making them understand that their deployment was both a deterrent and a precaution required another chunk of time.

"I get that we pretend it's an exercise, but what do we do if something really happens?" an ambulance driver asked.

"You do your job," Tom said, growing impatient. "It's not a drill anymore."

"And we're there to make sure people don't panic and start running around," the Fire Department captain said.

"Correct. And lead the hotel evacuation if needed. I hope it won't come to that. You're on the front line because your presence is reassuring. You don't have guns."

The captain shot Tom a lopsided smile. "We can't inflame the situation."

Sheriff Mayer guffawed. Tom was reminded he hadn't had a cigarette in ages.

"Let's get going," Tom said.

He returned to the Dodge. Billie wasn't in Giancana's car. Tom had already committed to drive Vivian and Muriel. It looked like he should add a blonde to the cargo. The trifecta. Pete Delgado would have a laughing fit. Al Matteotti would take bets. And Rachel would never, ever again let him leave town without her.

21. Wednesday, May 7

"Hey, Queenie." Abati squeezed her right breast.

"Jesus Christ, Mike, your hand is cold as ice." She couldn't possibly sleep knowing the Eraser might make his move any minute. "I'm tired. Play with yourself for a change."

She'd unplugged a lamp and set it by the side of the bed. It was something she could bash against Gomma's bald head if he got past the guards at the door. Damn, if only she had a gun. She was surrounded by heavies who clanked when they walked. Why the hell couldn't she lay her hands on a heater?

"Get dressed and go find Leo. I don't know these boys outside and I don't trust them."

"Your best guy is blotto in some corner with his pants down."

"Get him here. And where's Aldo? That idiot. You're the only one I can count on, and I ain't kidding." Abati put his hairy toes on her hip and pushed her to the edge of the bed.

"Okay, I'll go." She didn't feel right being naked in bed while Gomma roamed the corridors, anyway.

She dressed quickly and went to the sitting room. She didn't want to be seen by the bodyguards outside the door. She opened the window to the fire escape, hoping Gomma wasn't perched out there like a buzzard. The exit was clear. After removing the screen again, she ran down the steps in her bare feet. She scampered to the first black Caddy she saw in the parking lot, jerked open the unlocked passenger door, and found a snub-nosed .38 in the glove compartment. Finally, something she could work with. The gun was fully loaded, but there were no spare rounds among the roadmaps and cigarette packs. She slipped the pistol into the pocket of her suit jacket and trotted to the side entrance on the ground floor of the hotel.

She took the stairs and ran along the fourth-floor corridor to the suite. The room reeked of smoke, booze, and sex. A few bodies were sprawled on the sofas, but most attendees had stumbled back to their rooms. She was tempted to go up the staircase to check if the Gizzo thugs who'd brutalized her were still around. The pistol in her pocket whispered at her. *One in each head, Gunny.* She shook the thought away. Leo was in the armchair where she last saw him. The blonde was gone. Vivian took aim and punched him in the solar plexus. He came to his senses with a strangled gasp.

"Mike needs you, Leo. Gather yourself and fix your clothes. You're a disgrace."

He rubbed his stomach and grimaced. "Don't know what was in that booze. Never hurt like that."

"Come on, tough guy. The boss has little patience."

"I gotta get my pistol from my room."

"You're not armed at all times? What kind of bodyguard are you?"

"We're not armed in here."

Unbelievable. Not only were they smashed beyond belief, but they left the artillery behind. How had Abati survived this long? Some gunsels. She pulled the snubby out of her pocket. With reluctance, she handed it to Leo. "Mike needs you now. Let's go."

"What the hell are you doing with that? Dames can't handle a pistol with that much pop. Where'd you get it? You didn't have it when you arrived. I felt you up and checked your luggage. You were clean."

"Glad to hear the hooch hasn't pickled your memory. I found the gun. It's loaded. It's yours. Let's move. There's a killer on the loose. The Eraser. Heard of him?"

"He's after the boss?"

"He was after Giancana, but Giancana's gone, and Mike is holding the fort for him. Come on."

Leo looked at her as if she was speaking in tongues. He found some life in his limbs and got to his feet.

On the way to the second floor they ran into June Cavendish. She wore a white robe over her bathing suit, and held a pink rubber swimming cap. A hint of dawn glimmered through the hotel windows.

"Bad time for a swim, June," Vivian said. "Go back to your room and lock the door."

"What are you talking about? I always swim at dawn."

"That's a terrible idea. Please, go home."

"You're out of your mind, or drunk, or something." June hurried down the stairs to the ground floor.

"No one ever listens to me," Vivian said.

"Why would they? You're just a dumb broad."

Vivian had plenty to say about dumb. She also knew that no matter how hard she punched his stubborn head she'd never set Leo straight.

They reached the end of the second-floor hallway. The scene froze them in place. The thugs guarding Giancana's room lay dead on the floor. The carpet would have to be replaced.

"Fuck our luck," Vivian said. "He's in there."

Unless he was gone. Either way, Mike Abati was likely dead. The pinch in her heart was unexpected. She was in bed with him a few minutes ago.

Apart from the bodies, the hallway was empty. No one in the other rooms had rushed into the hall at the sound of gunfire. Gomma must have used a silenced pistol. A room service cart was parked near the door. The guards should have seen through that hoary ruse. Trafficante's boys were not as smart as their boss thought they were.

Pistol drawn, Leo rushed the door before Vivian could urge caution. She was two steps behind him, to the side, her instinct taking over. Never, never, attack straight on. The instant Leo crashed in, he took two quick shots to the chest. Vivian was knocked to the floor when Leo fell back into her. His weight crushed her hip and she yelped in pain. The bullets hadn't passed through his meaty hulk. If Gomma had been carrying a heavy Colt, like Tom, she'd be choking on her own blood. She was stuck under Leo, with Gomma looking at her. He wore a hotel service uniform. The man was fond of disguises. A professional good at his job. Resourceful. Creative.

She wished she'd killed him four years ago.

"Where is Giancana?" Gomma leveled the automatic at her. It was a Colt, but the light, hammerless pocket model. The long silencer made the thing less pocketable.

Vivian squeezed from under Leo's body. She had a side view of the suite. The bedroom door was open. Abati hung over the side of the bed, bleeding from a long gash on the head. It didn't look like a bullet wound. Gomma must have clobbered him with the butt of his pistol. Professional, indeed. He checked that he had the right mobster in residence. He wasn't paid to take out Abati.

"I don't know," Vivian said. "Maybe you should have asked Mike before you knocked him senseless."

"I don't need your advice." Gomma raised the pistol. "Gunselle."

He spared Abati but he wouldn't spare her. She was worse than competition. She was a hunter. He must know about the Bugsy contract. Imagine that, going all the way to Kansas City on a fucking FBI job and bumping into him.

An ear-splitting scream erupted in the hallway. Gomma leaned out of the door. His gun remained trained on Vivian. She saw an unfamiliar woman standing in the doorway of some mobster's room, her hands on her cheeks, hollering. Gomma looked at Vivian. She knew that look. She rolled to the side as a bullet splintered the wooden floor a couple inches from her head. She scrambled back to the protection of Leo's body. She peeked over the dead man like a soldier over a sandbag. Gomma hurried into the hallway. He shot the screaming woman in the face, at close range. Her head slammed against the wall, brains and blood everywhere. The sudden silence felt like air had been sucked out of the world. Vivian charged into the suite, slipped in Leo's blood, and landed face down. With a glance back at her, Gomma ran down the corridor and disappeared.

A man appeared in the doorway where the woman had slumped to the floor. He stared at the mess on the wall, at the blood soaking the carpet runner, at Vivian lying half in the room, half in the corridor. There were four bodies by Giancana's suite now and chaos was moments away.

Sure enough, doors opened and men with handguns filled the hallway.

"What the fuck?" One tough guy glowered at Vivian. "Did you do this?"

"With what? My hair pins?" She leaned on the wall to get up and left a bloody handprint there. Leo's blood. "A hitman was after Giancana, but he and Trafficante were gone when the killer showed up. Mike Abati and I, and the muscle, we were bait. And look what happened."

"Where's the shooter?"

Vivian pointed at the end of the corridor.

She resisted telling them Gizzo was behind it. It would start a massacre. Giancana said Gizzo was his. He could be counted on to deliver retribution. None of this was her concern. She went to the bedroom to check on Abati. He was coming around. Vivian helped him back onto the bed. She pressed a corner of the bedsheet to his battered head. As thick as his skull was, he'd be okay.

She kissed him on the forehead. "You should treat your girls better," she muttered. "It won't make you less of a man, *paisano*."

He moaned. "Queenie?"

"I gotta go, baby. Take care. Maybe we'll have a drink some day."

He reached for her but she was too fast for him.

Leo still clutched the .38. She peeled it from his hand. It hadn't been fired.

The hallway was filled with loud, angry men. Lots of shouting and waving of guns, but not much concrete action. Vivian pushed through the crowd in the direction Gomma had taken. How much time had passed? Five minutes? He must be gone by now. She had to go to Muriel and Aldo and find Tom.

"Queenie?"

Billie stood in the open door of room 205, wearing the travel clothes she had on earlier. A fat leather purse hung from her shoulder.

Vivian sighed. What made her everybody's guardian suddenly? She had enough to worry about without the blonde. Tom's lusty blonde, damn it!

"You want out of here, Billie? Come on."

The woman hurried behind Vivian.

They were running down the stairs when Vivian recognized the two goons who treated her like garbage at the party. They were coming to check on the noises. Unless Gizzo sent them to make sure Giancana was cold. Vivian wished she could throw them to the rabid dogs upstairs.

She couldn't keep her fury inside. "You are dead," she barked. "Giancana will come for all of you."

The men stopped, surprised. One of them pulled his gun and fired, without bothering to aim. Vivian ducked and the bullet shattered a crystal sconce. The shot was deafening. She felt Billie grab her arm and propel her down the remaining steps. The man fired again, but by then they were running and the shot went wide. Vivian squeezed off two shots in the direction of the staircase but couldn't see if she'd hit anything.

Billie pulled her along, and she wasn't delicate about it. Vivan spun and grabbed the blonde's arm. She changed their direction, navigating them toward the spa, toward Muriel and Aldo, and the back way out to the parking lot.

Suddenly, lights came on, with an orchestra of screams and yells, the sound of running on stairs. People seemed to be pouring out of every door. The entire hotel was up in arms.

As they passed the bar and restaurant, red lights splashed on the marble of the lobby like a mirrored ball above a dance floor.

Vivian blinked. The police? So fast? She wanted to stick her fingers in her ears to clear the cotton the gunshots stuffed in there.

They darted through the spa entrance and emerged in the pool area lit by the emergency beacons. Vivian was in the lead now. The steam and the heat stopped her like a fist. She couldn't find enough air to fill her lungs. She leaned against the tile wall to get her breath back.

"You said you had a car." Billie was gasping too. "The parking lot isn't this way."

"In the back, past the outdoor pool. Do you see Aldo and Muriel? It's like I'm in an aquarium." Her hearing was clearing up.

"They're probably where we left them." Billie pointed. "Over there, on the other side, by that potted palm tree."

Vivian pushed herself away from the wall and heard the steady strokes of someone swimming in the pool. Really? People were painting walls with brains and dyeing carpets with blood, and somebody was swimming laps? She walked to the glowing perimeter lights of the pool and saw a woman's lithe form glide by. June fucking Cavendish and her pink swimming cap. Vivian stood transfixed. Regular life floated by while whores and reprobates died upstairs.

Billie joined her by the side of the pool. "Is that the woman who fixed Muriel's black eye? She has the right attitude. If everybody jumped in the pool, we could have some fun instead of all that shit."

"You spent most of the night in your bathing suit."

"And here I am, back at the beginning," Billie said. "Where did you find that gun?"

The pistol hung by Vivian's side. "I forgot I was holding it. Have you seen Tom?"

"Not since he walked me to Sam's floor. He said he had a job to do."

Vivian took a deep breath. "His car is outside. I wish I'd taken a minute to straighten out the plan with him."

Billie took a step toward her. "He's a cop. Are you …"

The shot was muffled by a suppressor but it still echoed off the tile. Billie let out a cry and collapsed. Vivian raised the pistol. She couldn't see the shooter through the fog. She heard water cascade on the edge of the pool and pointed the gun in that direction. Was Gomma shooting from the pool?

June climbed the ladder.

Vivian exhaled. She had been a hair away from

plugging the Avon woman. "Get back in the water. There's a killer in the mist." She crouched and felt for Billie with her free hand. "Where did he get you?"

The voice was a murmur. "My leg's burning."

Billie's thigh was sticky. Blood pumped out of a ragged hole. Vivian thought *femoral artery, she doesn't have much time*. Then a hand pushed hers out of the way.

"I have this." June reached for a robe thrown on a lounger and pulled the terrycloth belt through the loops. In no time, she had a tourniquet in place. "What are you waiting for? What do you have a gun for?"

Vivian felt like she'd been slapped. She moved behind a pillar, away from the two women. Billie moaned.

Vivian squinted at the palm tree in its pot, a phantom plant in the vapors. If Muriel and Aldo were over there, they didn't make a move. They must have left. Damn Aldo, he was supposed to be good at following orders.

A shot swished. Vivian felt her arm give way. She dropped the pistol.

She bent down and reached for the gun with her left hand but it slid across the tile toward the edge of the pool. It slid across the tile because Gomma had kicked it. She saw his feet at the same time she felt his arm around her neck. He pulled her up and slammed her against the pillar. Her injured arm connected, and she cursed.

Out of the mist. The bastard came out of the mist.

"I knew it was you when I saw Abati on the train." Even in the warm air, she could feel his hot humid breath in her ear, the pistol's mouth kissing her skull, the brutal pain in her arm making her eyes water. "I've seen your Hollywood head shots." He chuckled. "Head shots. How ironic. I was offered the job of taking you out once. Something called honor made me refuse."

"Gee, thanks." Vivian's voice cracked under the pressure of his arm on her throat. "You can let me go."

"Not this time. When I saw you on the train, I thought you'd quit the business and gotten another job. Gone straight, so to speak. As a mobster's whore. Then I wondered if you were after Giancana too, a little insurance for Gizzo in case I fucked up. Then I thought you might be after me, since you missed your chance after Bugsy Siegel, but that wasn't likely, us meeting on the train like that. I watched you give yourself to these men during the orgy and I knew the score." He pressed the muzzle harder against her skull.

"You're right." She winced at the searing pain in her arm. "I'm just a whore."

"Wrong," said Gomma. "You're a dead whore."

Vivian relaxed into herself. A bullet through the skull would ease the suffering in her arm. And every other suffering in her life. Maggie would be taken care of and she was relieved Tom wouldn't see her fall. She prepared herself, like she'd watched so many men do.

The sound of a gunshot rang off the tile, loud, and she felt something wet slide down her neck. Gomma's arm slipped from around her throat as his weight fell off her back, and she stumbled forward, looking down at his bald head. His eyes stared at her through the wisps of mist and his blood drained toward the pool. Vivian almost went over the edge. The warm water looked inviting. A bath would make her whole again. Wash the blood and gore away.

Suddenly all the lights came on, blinding like the flash of a camera. Gomma's blood was the color of tomato sauce. His pink head looked obscene. Vivian teetered on her bare feet. Her dirty feet, splattered with brownish blood. She was an orphan on the farm again. She felt herself swoon and a strong arm caught her.

"I'm sorry, Queenie," Aldo said. "I didn't see him come in. After the first shot, I had a good fix, and he slipped away, damn weasel. Are you okay? Your arm …"

The bullet hit her about three inches above the wrist. She couldn't move her fingers. They hung there, useless, dripping blood.

"It's just an arm. Billie …" She leaned on him.

Billie was on the tile floor, her head in Muriel's lap.

She was sickly pale, her face coated in sweat, but the bleeding had stopped.

June removed her rubber swim cap. She held a towel and wrapped it around Vivian's forearm. She snapped the chin strap of her cap to hold the improvised bandage in place.

"We have to get you to a hospital."

"You're not a nurse anymore, June. You push lipstick. It's a square life. Safe."

"Safe? Look around."

Vivian thought the pool area could use a good hose down. "This place is a shooting gallery and I haven't killed anything. I'm a pathetic excuse for a gunslinger."

The clapping sound of running feet rang in the echo chamber of the swimming pool. A smile formed on Vivian's face. He was back. A bit late. But when were cops ever on time?

"Where the fuck have you been, Tommy?"

June stepped between them, her eyes on him. "We have to get them to a hospital."

"The emergency people are preoccupied right now. Crowd and damage control. Get her out of here. Take my car." Tom tossed the keys to Aldo. "A blue Dodge, Missouri plates. In the back parking lot. Go with them, June. Please." He reached in his pocket and extracted a card that he gave to Aldo. "You'll hit a check point. Show them this card."

"What is it?"

"*Carte blanche. Laissez Passer*. Whatever. It will get you through. Go to KC. Find the Williams Garage. It's two blocks from Union Station. There's a map on the front seat. Ben Williams, the owner's son, lives over the shop. Tell him Tom Keegan sent you. Ben knows a friendly doctor. I'll meet you there."

"Billie lost a lot of blood," June said. "She might go into shock."

"There isn't room for all of us in the car. I'll take care of Billie." Tom went down on his knees next to the blonde, taking over from Muriel. Billie reached for him.

"Of course," Vivian muttered. Her protest lacked bite, the pain was eating at her.

Billie rolled her head from side to side. Her eyes were open. She was staring at Tom. Vivian wanted to scream and couldn't.

"Enough talking. Let's scram." Aldo held a hand out to Muriel and pulled her up. "I'm sick of this place."

"Give me your gun," Tom said. "It's a murder weapon now."

Aldo shook his head. "No way I'm going naked, pal."

"Take mine." Vivian pointed with her chin. "The snubby down there."

Aldo retrieved the pistol at the edge of the pool. "There's gas in the car?"

"More than enough for KC. Get the girls over there in one piece, kid."

"I'm a good driver. I'll look after them."

June slipped her beltless robe over her swimsuit. She knelt and brushed her hand against Billie's cheek.

Vivian glanced back at Tom and Billie as Aldo led the women around the pool to a set of French doors. The doors led to the garden. The irises stood erect at dawn.

They skirted the outdoor pool. The parking lot access door hung open, the Dodge was parked next to it. Aldo helped Vivian into the back with June. He took the wheel and Muriel sat next to him.

The big hotel was fully illuminated now. Vivian thought the party going on in there was as warped as the *Lieutenants' Ball*. She swore she would not set foot in The Elms ever again.

The car sped away, leaving behind the red lights of fire trucks, ambulances, and police cruisers.

Vivian leaned against June in the back seat. Her arm, in June's lap, was on fire. Maybe she'd take a slug of morphine. Just this once. The droning of the car calmed her. She watched the faces of Aldo and Muriel in the oncoming headlights.

"Were you an emergency room nurse, June?" she said.

"You can call it that. I served on Bataan. Three months of endless casualties." June's voice had gone remote. It matched the darkness that surrounded the car.

"I heard that was hell on earth."

"Try to rest," June said.

The car seemed to move on a very soft cloud.

22. Wednesday, May 7

"They're gone?" Billie muttered.

"Just you and me now, babe. I'm going to lift you, and it'll hurt. Ready?"

"Where are we going?"

"There's an ambulance in front of the hotel. You'll be on your way to Kansas City in no time. Blood transfusion. All that good stuff."

"Not for me. I'm Sam's property. Everybody knows it." She leaned back in Tom's lap. "The cops will be all over me. Pushing to break me."

"I'm a cop."

Her chuckle turned into a painful cough. "Sam will get to me, Tom. I know too much. That nurse should have let me bleed."

She tried to reach for the tourniquet and he stopped her hand.

"Okay. No hospital. We're going road running. You trust me?"

"If I say I do ... sounds like I'm committing to something else."

He wiped the sweat off her face before kissing her. "If you die on me, Billie, I'll be very upset. Ready?"

She nodded. "... take my purse. I bleed for what's in there."

Tom picked up the handbag, put an arm under her shoulders and the other in the crook of her knees, and lifted her. The pain must have been terrible. She didn't make a sound but her head flopped over his arm. She had fainted. Maybe that was for the best.

He stepped around Gomma's body and hurried through the spa, into the hallway, toward the main lobby.

A crowd in pajamas and nightgowns blocked the exit. They chattered, milled about, questioned hotel employees, surrounded the firemen. They were more curious and eager for information than anxious. It didn't matter if they were Mob or

Avon. To Tom, carrying unconscious Billie, they all blended together in an unmoving mass.

"Is she dead?"

A woman's shrill voice. He turned to face her. He knew her. She was the fragile-looking blonde who looked like Veronica Lake. He'd seen her with Vivian and the other one, the creole girl with the Medusa stare.

As if the thought had summoned her, Jasmine stepped forward.

"He nailed her?" she said.

"He tried. She won't make it if I can't get out of here." Lying to her didn't seem like a good idea.

"Even if you do." She made a face. "Between the cops and the hoods ..."

Tom nodded. The crowd was thick in front of him. Billie felt warm in his arms, but it might be a fever heat, and shivers would follow. He mouthed. "Help me."

Jasmine threw her head back and bellowed. "The killer went for Momo. He failed and took his woman instead." She yelled. "He killed Billie! Let the dead pass!"

It was theatrical, over-the-top, and effective. A roar came from the crowd and a path opened in front of Tom. Women grabbed hankies, men crossed themselves. He glanced at Jasmine. She winked. Then she raised both arms and let out a shriek that would have shamed a banshee.

Tom didn't wait to see what happened next, he rushed through the hotel's front doors. He needed a car. Preferably not a police cruiser. He couldn't bring the cops to Ben Williams's doorstep.

"Tom!"

A man separated from a cluster of smokers huddled next to a planter. Tom caught the light reflecting off a glass bottle. In the middle of the mayhem, somebody had raided the bar.

Mark Jorgenson, Avon Sales.

He leaned toward the unconscious Billie. "I know her. I told her she should change her lipstick color. Because of her skin tone. She's not a real blonde." Jorgenson slurred his words. He touched Billie's cheek. "She's alive."

"I need to get her out of here, Mark."

Jorgenson pointed at the red-flashing ambulance.

Tom shook his head.

Jorgenson dropped his cigarette and crushed it underfoot. He patted his suit pockets and extracted a key ring. "I have a car but you'll have to drive. I had a few too many."

Jorgenson was sober enough to remember where he'd parked. The car was a sensible Ford Coupe. "There's a blanket in the trunk. I'll sit in the back with her. Keep her from bouncing around."

They arranged Billie on the bench seat and Jorgenson put an arm around her and her head in his lap.

"I wish she'd come to." Tom slipped behind the wheel.

Jorgenson felt for Billie's pulse. "Slight but steady. It looks like the bullet went through."

Tom eased the car through the parking lot. "It did serious damage on the way."

A police car sat at the lot exit and a trooper flagged them down. Tom rolled down his window. He showed his badge and one of Detective Campbell's cards. The cop glanced at both and saluted.

"Do you need an escort, sir?"

"Is Sheriff Mayer still at the intersection?"

"Yes, Mr. Keegan. Do you want me to radio ahead?"

"That would be helpful. Thank you." Tom put the car in gear.

Jorgenson whistled. "I didn't think Avon had that kind of pull. You're FBI?"

"Just a cop."

Sheriff Mayer's checkpoint was now a roadblock. Tom slowed down but one of the cars across the road pulled back to let him pass through. He waved through the open car window and a uniformed cop signaled that he was good to go.

"Where are we taking her?"

"Kansas City."

"Half an hour," Jorgenson said. "It'll be tight. She's burning with fever."

The Ford was a lot slower than Ben Williams's Dodge. Tom grabbed the wheel so hard that his knuckles hurt. He willed the car to swallow the miles. When he looked in the rearview mirror, he couldn't see Billie's face, only Jorgenson leaning over her.

A faint pulsating glow on the horizon hinted at KC's existence.

"Did Gomma do this?" Jorgenson said.

Tom blinked. He gave a quick glance at the mirror. Jorgenson looked relaxed, casual. Tom released his grip on the steering wheel and changed position slightly to make the Colt in the shoulder holster more accessible. It wouldn't make a crumb of difference if Jorgenson had a gun aimed at his spine.

"Who's Gomma?" he said.

Jorgenson laughed. "Very funny. The man the sheriff set a roadblock for. A sheriff you know by name. Seriously, Tom, we're on the same side." He sighed. "I think we are."

"Billie was in the wrong place." Another look at the rearview mirror. Jorgenson was nodding. "Who are you, Mark?"

"Avon Sales." A chuckle. "Like you're Avon Production. You're good, I never even thought you might be a cop. You have a cigarette? I don't want to dig for mine."

Tom handed him his pack and lighter over the seat. "Who are you working for?"

The lights of Kansas City were a lot closer now. They might be ten minutes away from the Williams Garage.

"Hush hush, can't tell."

It was an answer. Tom had encountered a few shadowy types in the last months of the war, in that aftermath when unholy alliances were in the making, when enemies became useful, if not respectable, and friends turned inconvenient. That Mark Jorgenson with his boyish good looks and easy charm belonged to that dubious phalanx was not a complete shock. Deception was an art and he was certainly talented. The surprise was that he shed the mask.

"Why are you breaking cover?" Tom said.

"I want to know what happened."

"Billie is hurt and if she goes to the hospital a squad of law enforcement types will swoop on her, and the man she works for will make sure she doesn't utter a word."

"Is Gomma loose?"

"No."

Jorgenson blew smoke toward the open car window. "Where's Giancana?"

"I don't know."

"You're helping his woman escape. That's worth something."

Jorgenson was silent the rest of the way.

Tom parked in front of the garage, behind the Dodge Coronet, and Jorgenson helped him get Billie out of the car. Tom was about to go up the stairs to Ben Williams's apartment when Aldo appeared.

"Is the doctor there?"

Aldo nodded.

"Take her upstairs," Tom said. "I'll be there soon."

Mark Jorgenson was leaning on the car, smoking. He was as unperturbed as if he'd been among the Avon meeting attendees. He handed his pack of cigarettes back to Tom and gave him a light with his own lighter.

"Tell me if I have this right," Tom said. "Gomma was on a government contract."

"Something tells me you're not a traffic cop." Jorgenson smiled. "We worked it through the Gizzo organization. It isn't hard to make people believe they came up with the idea."

"Especially when it's something they've been chewing on for a while."

"Between opportunity and motive. I don't think you're on the take, yet you orchestrated Giancana's exit. Why?"

"Giancana dies and we have a bloodbath on our hands."

"You wanted to avoid a gang war? Noble and wrongheaded. Thinning out the goon population makes our cities safer. I won't weep for dead criminals. The less of them, the better."

Tom shook his head. "I'm a homicide detective. I arrest murderers, I don't encourage them. No matter who the victim is."

Jorgenson puffed on his cigarette. "A fine philosophical position. Not practical if you want results."

"Five people died at The Elms tonight and two were injured. It would have been much worse if Sam Giancana had been killed. An innocent woman is among the dead. Billie might not survive and a friend of mine was hurt. Have you ever been in a gunfight, Mark?"

"I served." He sighed. "I was never on the frontline."

"It's nothing to brag about. There's confusion, anxiety, fear, panic, detachment …" Tom dropped his cigarette and stepped on it. "You lay out fire. Nobody shoots straight. Except snipers. They have what nobody else has: time. Donato Gomma was a sniper. Everybody else just scrambles. It isn't pretty, Mark. It isn't orderly. And it's damn unpredictable." He leaned on the hood of the Ford. "I hate that."

Jorgenson walked to the driver side door. "Giancana might be a thorn in our side sometime in the future."

"Get a warrant. I'll help you arrest him."

The Ford did a U-turn and tore down the street. Tom didn't wave goodbye.

23. Thursday, May 8...and a few days later

It was only two blocks to the train station but Ben Williams insisted on driving them in the Dodge Coronet. Vivian claimed her stitched, wrapped, and splinted arm wasn't a bother. As if it wasn't obvious she was hurting. Tom accepted Ben's offer against her protests. He understood that she needed to uphold her tough image, and after several rounds of morphine before, during, and after the surgery, she had grown wary of the easy comfort it provided. Tom thought the two-day train trip would test her resilience enough.

They were two hours out of Kansas City and Vivian was asleep in the lower bunk of the sleeper cabin. Tom had stayed by her side, making light conversation, until her regular breathing confirmed she'd given in to the strain of the past forty-eight hours. He was too wound up to do the same. He stood in the hallway, smoking, undisturbed except for occasional passengers stumbling back to their compartments after a few drinks in the bar car.

There was nothing to see through the windows. The landscape was uniformly dark. The only points of light were the reflection of his lit cigarette and the hallway sconces. The events of the past two days rolled like a jumpy film reel on the black canvas of the train window.

The scene at the pool with Billie and Gomma on the blood-stained tile. Jasmine screaming in the lobby. The morally ambiguous conversation with Mark Jorgenson in front of the Williams Garage. The scramble in Ben Williams's apartment, reminiscent of a frontline hospital, down to the morphine syrettes, transfusion rig, and improvised bandages. Ben's family doctor had called upon wartime reflexes, as had June Cavendish in her gore-splattered bathrobe. Professionals calm under pressure. Ben's two-bedroom apartment was crowded but everybody behaved. With the exception of Vivian who went after the elderly doctor when he suggested that the women should be in a hospital under police supervision. He meant that they should be handcuffed to the bed rail. One look at Aldo and Muriel, and the man must have been reminded of Bonnie and Clyde. Tom's badge brought the temperature down, even if the doctor wasn't entirely convinced. San Francisco PD. Why not the Texas Rangers?

Tom smiled at his reflection in the train window. It was true that their bedraggled group looked more like a gang of criminals than the real mobsters who wore impeccable handmade suits and rode in glossy Cadillacs. Sam Giancana and Sonny Trafficante must be plotting revenge. Gizzo and his crew prepared for the backlash. Mike Abati was two goons and a moll short, but he jumped a few rungs on the syndicate ladder. Big Mike got something out of the Kansas City fiasco.

All the police could put in the credit column was Donato Gomma's death, and they'd had no hand in it. Aldo shot the Eraser and saved Vivian's life, another professional assassin. She was winged, so maybe that could be counted as a positive too. Tom hoped Aldo was smart enough to choose a new career.

The kid had left with Muriel. "By the first train out," he told Tom. "Don't care where it goes. I hope it works out. She's a doll." He shook Tom's hand. "Can't believe I gave my rod to a cop."

Tom had given Aldo's gun to Ben Williams, for protection. The young man took it to the garage and hammered it to pieces.

"I don't want Billie to see it," he said. "She's been around guns too much." Lying in bed next to the beautiful blonde—for the transfusion—did something to Ben Williams. "We're bonded by blood. We both have a bad leg. Maybe she'll stick around for a while."

Tom wished them the best. Ben's solid hands would be kept full with Billie.

The thought made Tom even more anxious to get home. Two days. He had called Rachel from Union Station, when he was sure nothing would come in the way. She said she believed him this time. Tom was confident his report to the chief at SFPD would never be typed. It was doubtful his presence at The Elms would ever be questioned. He was listed as an Avon attendee, and so was Mark Jorgenson whose credentials were as bogus as his own.

June Cavendish showed up at the garage on Thursday afternoon. She wanted to see how Billie was doing and she brought both Tom's and Vivian's luggage.

"I checked you out," June said. "On Avon's tab. I shouldn't have bothered. The hotel is a circus."

"I was about to go shopping for Vivian," Tom said. "How did you manage to get her things?"

"I said it was my room. There wasn't anybody around to say otherwise. All the gangsters have flown the coop. Her purse is in the case." She handed Tom a cardboard box. "I put together a sampler. A parting gift, courtesy of Avon. It's mostly women's products, but I stuck a few from our men's catalog in there for you."

Tom met a few good people on this trip. He wasn't sure what to think of Mark Jorgenson. He leaned on the window, felt the rhythm of the train wheels. He should try to sleep.

Last smoke. He lit a fresh cigarette from the stub of the old one.

*

Vivian stayed in the cabin. The jostling of the train, the crucible of the gangways, and having to weave between passengers, put too much strain on her arm sling and makeshift cast.

She tried though. She was determined to go to the restaurant car. Tom helped her clean up and get dressed. She applied a dab of make-up, and he laced her oxfords. They made it to the end of the car and she was in tears.

"I could carry you," he said.

"In the first curve, we'll bump into something and I'll howl."

"We have …"

"No."

June Cavendish had packed two morphine syrettes in the Avon kit, just in case. When Tom unwrapped the bandages to clean the wound, the damage caused by their trip down the hallway was clear to see. Two stitches were torn.

"It isn't worth it," he said. "I'll bring back lunch."

"And a little wine?"

Ben Williams's family doctor would disapprove but he was miles away. "One glass, with food, and then you lie down again."

A generous tip ensured food delivery for the remainder of the journey. Tom didn't wander around to kill time. There was no reason for it and nothing to see that was more interesting than the landscape out of the compartment window. He only stepped out to stretch his legs and grab a smoke. Vivian dozed and they talked. Of her childhood, a little. It was unpleasant and she didn't dwell on it. She brushed lightly over her Hollywood years, went deeper on her truck-driving stints during and after the war. Then she switched to Maggie, and Otis, the bartender at Pepper's Swing Club. And she quizzed Tom.

"There's nothing that colorful in my background," he said.

He told her about his parents, who'd just moved to San Diego, and about his sister who used to work for the SFPD but was now a teacher in Modesto. "She and her husband are expecting a baby, in July, I believe."

"Have you ever thought of doing another job?"

"I was on my way to law school when the war happened. My head was in a different place when I came back. I think I'm useful where I am."

"You like following orders?"

"I work for a good man. He's political, all police chiefs are, but he keeps me out of that sticky mud. Early this year, I was detached to the LAPD for a few weeks. Let's say, politely, that if I was a detective down there, I would have gone back to practicing law by now."

And so they passed the time. The undercurrent of seduction was always present, the electricity, the nagging sexual need. Without the barrier of the broken arm and the pain, tension in the compartment would have been unbearable. Tom would probably have retreated to the hallway or the lounge, and Vivian would have resented it with all the force of her very resolute mind.

The train was rolling into Sacramento when she said: "You've decided that you'll never sleep with me. Is that it, Tommy?"

"Six years ago, it would have been a different story. I'm convinced it wouldn't have ended well. For me." He got up. "I'll get us a drink. It's about that time of day, and we'll be home soon."

Tom had been in the police business long enough, and war before that, to know that everybody was capable of killing if circumstances flipped the switch. Protecting those you love, protecting yourself, for a higher cause whatever that may be, blinded by passion, impaired, for kicks, by accident ... For Vivian, aka Gunselle, killing was a job. She killed like Tom's grandmother cut a chicken's head, without emotion, as a matter of course.

He could picture himself, his uniform in a duffel bag, running into Vivian in a train station, falling head over heels for her, then finding out what she was. The pain of that. The betrayal. The inevitable break-up. Maybe she'd even put a bullet in his head.

"What can I get you, sir?" the bartender said.

The train lurched forward. Home. Soon.

"A whiskey neat and a glass of red wine. Burgundy."

He held both glasses in one hand, a finger in the whiskey, and stumbled through the swinging cars and treacherous gangways. The man who opened the car door for him, helpful, was a bulky mass.

"Thank you."

Tom blinked. Black hat, black roomy suit, a thin tie with a silver pin. The smell of hair tonic. The teeth of a carnivore. Mike Abati.

"Ya welcome," Abati said, and went past Tom in the gangway.

A jolt threw Tom against the train windows. He didn't spill the drinks.

He opened the compartment door. They kept the curtains closed and that was a smart move. He handed the wine glass to Vivian and sat down.

"Abati's on the train."

"Fuck!" Then, a second later: "It doesn't matter."

"Agreed. But I'd rather not have him scream *Queenie* at the top of his lungs."

"Open my suitcase." She grinned. "I'll be your plain Jane wife."

"Can you?"

She leaned forward and planted a kiss on his mouth. "Watch me."

*

In Union Station, on arrival, Abati didn't spare them a glance. He cut through the crowd like a snowplow and bullied his way to the head of the taxi line. Tom and Vivian watched from a distance.

"He's rushing to report to Lima," she said.

"Let's go around the corner, we'll have a better chance to snatch a cab."

"You're impatient. Rachel's waiting."

"You need to see a doctor. I don't know if we can find a clinic open this late." He waved at a taxi headed for the line.

"Take the cab," Vivian said. "You're in a hurry. I have a doctor who answers her phone at all hours. It comes with the territory. With a hefty fee."

"I'll take you. What's her address?"

"She wouldn't like me giving it out to a cop."

He leaned close to the driver and gave him an address.

Vivian was stunned. "You know where I live?"

"Get in."

He helped her, making sure she landed softly, then sat down next to her. When the cab stopped in front of her building, he told the driver to keep the meter running. He carried her suitcase inside and held out his hand for the key. She gave him her purse.

"In the side pocket," she said, in a low voice.

She glanced at her mailbox in the lobby. It was full, Maggie hadn't bothered with the mail. Tom found the box key on the ring and grabbed a clump of envelopes. He preceded her to the elevator, into the car, pushed the button, and up they went. To her floor. To her door. They stood together outside for a moment like a shy couple returning from a first date. A fun evening on the town. Wondering what might come next. Tom unlocked the door. The place was empty.

"Do you know where Maggie's playing tonight?" he said.

Vivian shook her head. "Her schedule is on the calendar next to the phone." Maggie. He must have followed Maggie ... That's how he knew where she lived. She felt weird. Defenseless? As if she'd walked in to find a stranger sitting on her sofa, having a drink.

Tom carried her suitcase into the apartment and put it down next to the phone table. He dropped the mail and switched on the small desk lamp. He studied the calendar. "Pepper's, of course. I'll have somebody stop by and tell Maggie you're home and need help."

"Leave her alone, Tom. I'll call my doctor. She'll come get me."

"You're sure?"

"It won't be the first time. You go to Rachel. She must be desperate to hold you."

He landed a kiss on the top of her head. "Goodnight, Vivian. I won't bother you again. Stay out of trouble."

She nodded. "Thanks for seeing me home."

The whole sequence of events was unreal. After he closed the door, she made the phone call, dialing awkwardly with her left hand. She hung up and went through the mail. A letter was addressed to Margaret Bates. From the Department of State. She put the envelope in the pocket of her suit, sat in an armchair, and waited for Dr. Smith.

Maybe her brain would be working again by the time the physician arrived.

*

A newspaper, like a police station, is never completely quiet. There are no drunks yelling from a holding cell but voices are loud to cover the racket. Tom knew the way to the newsroom. He tipped his hat at the night watchman.

"Haven't seen you in a while, Mr. Keegan," the man said. "I think she's still up there."

Of course she was. Unless they had a date, Rachel clocked long hours. Always something to look up, something to follow up on. She might not have as tall a work stack as he did, but she was as committed to see the bottom of it.

A couple of reporters were hammering at typewriters in the newsroom. They didn't look up when Tom walked in. Rachel's desk was in a corner with half a view from half a window. It was a privilege, recognition for her byline. She'd worked hard for that half window. Tom doubted she looked out of it much.

He was next to the desk closest to hers when she spotted movement from the corner of her eye. She was out of her chair and in his arms before he could take one more step.

"You made it," she muttered.

He kissed her and his hands were all over her as if he needed to make certain she was made of solid material.

Rachel came up for air. "Give me a m…" Barely enough air for the next round. "Okay, you …" She laughed. "How many hands do you have?"

"I wish I had more." He held her as he reached for her purse on the desk. "I have a taxi downstairs. Let's go home."

The cab driver watched them get in and whistled. "Man, you have some life …"

"Just. Drive."

*

Rachel had questions, an entire phone book of them.

"Tomorrow," Tom said. "I promise."

He didn't carry her up the stairs, his third story was a bit much and he had a suitcase. He only let go of her hand when they were in the apartment. It seemed safe to set her free then. He posted her in the bathroom entrance.

"I spent two days and two nights on a train. I need a shower. Stay right there."

"I can make you a drink." She smiled.

"I don't want to take my eyes off you. Yes, I'm a little mad."

"It's only been a week, Tommy." She was on the verge of a laughing fit.

And what week that had been. "You have no idea, baby."

When she started taking her clothes off, he thought that maybe she had a pretty good idea after all.

Epilogue – Sunday, May 11

It was past nine and they hadn't bothered with coffee yet. They'd made love, too fast, slept, made love again, more leisurely, cuddled, which led to some lazy petting, fallen asleep, found more energy ... sex definitely had an elastic effect on the clock.

Tom felt rubbery, and not in a bouncy way. Rachel was all mussed up, surrounded by pillows. It took a massive effort to lift his suitcase onto the bed and pull stuff out for the cleaners.

"I've never seen you in that one," Rachel said, eying the wrinkled blue suit. "And what is that." She grabbed an Avon moisturizing lotion, opened it, and squeezed a dollop on the back of her hand. "Smells nice, feels good. I like a man who takes care of himself."

He had to tell her the story. He might as well start there. "They had an Avon conference in the hotel where I stayed. In Kansas City. A place called The Elms."

Rachel's eyes widened. "The shooting. I saw the news bulletin. Not much detail about the people who died. You were there? What for?"

He raised a warning finger. "Off the record."

She made a face. "As if you won't keep the juicy stuff under wraps anyway."

"A hitman had a contract on a notorious gangster in town for a Mob meeting. The killer was taken down but not before he shot some bodyguards. An innocent woman died too. It could have been worse. The Avon lady who put these samples in my suitcase was a nurse during the war. She saved a girl's life."

"What were you doing there?"

"Running an undercover agent. The feds had a plan to infiltrate the Mob proceedings. We tried to neutralize the hitman before he got on site but he slipped through. Imagine the scene. A packed hotel. Avon delegates on one side and armed mobsters on the other. Now add a professional assassin to the mix. It could have been a massacre." He shook his head. "We were very lucky."

"I like it better when you stay in town," Rachel said.

He fished the swim trunks out of the pile of laundry. "We could risk a trip south."

She snatched the shorts out of his hand. "Oh, I want to see you in these."

He laughed. "Nothing you haven't seen before." He pushed the clothes and the suitcase off the bed and moved close to her. "Before I left for Kansas City, I made a promise to myself, that when I came back ..." He shook his head. "I'm doing this wrong. It should be more formal, so we'll remember, years from now."

She pulled the bedsheet to cover herself. "Formal, like this?"

When they emerged, mid-afternoon, they went for a long walk in Golden Gate Park, had an early dinner at a small seafood restaurant on the waterfront, and when it started drizzling decided to catch a movie to cap the day. Rachel's choice, *Deadline - U.S.A.*, a newspaper story with crimes, was a perfect fit.

"Let's sit in the back row," Tom said.

"That's where the kids hide to misbehave."

"Yeah, I just chopped off half my age."

They snuggled as best they could on the plush seats after the usher and his indiscreet light had gone to check on potential sinners.

"If I fall asleep, don't let me snore." Tom couldn't remember the last time he felt so loose, yet so sober.

The newsreel unspooled.

Korea. Tom remembered the young airmen in Sacramento, future navigators. He hoped the entire mess would be over before they were deployed. The commentary weaved around terms like 'static war' and 'stalemate', words that didn't reflect the reality on the ground. An army didn't have to move to bleed. He tightened his grip on Rachel's shoulders.

The news moved to more pleasant topics. Truman waving to crowds. Was that Kansas City? Tom sat up. Long shots of cattle pens, crowds around barbecue stands, Truman again, on the podium, giving a speech, a shot of a Ferris wheel with people waving. The cameraman shot from below and made the contraption look a lot bigger than it was. Tom smiled. The image would make Vivian laugh.

And there she was, licking a drippy ice cream cone. Really licking.

Tom felt Rachel stiffen against him.

The sparse audience burst out laughing. Whistles, catcalls, a few obscene comments. Vivian's performance straddled a thin line between country innocence and censorship baiting. Tom knew what came next. The camera followed Vivian, her trim behind and swaying hips. She leaned over the ring toss game counter, two feet from him. Small mercies, he was only seen in profile, and briefly. The brim of his gray fedora, a birthday gift from Rachel, shaded his face. The photographer lingered lovingly on Vivian's curves.

Rachel pulled away from him with a shudder.

The movie reel ended, and people applauded. On to the cartoon. *Merrie Melodies*. *Little Red Rodent Hood*. Looked like a good one.

Rachel was half out of her seat. "You were with her!" She leaned over the armrest. "Don't tell me you bumped into her by accident."

The end of the sentence hissed in Tom's ears. A tiny mouse squeaked on screen.

"No, I …"

This wasn't the place for explanations. People laughed. Tom didn't see anything funny.

Rachel stood and hurried along the row of seats. Tom trotted behind her. She collided with the elderly usher standing in the aisle and the man dropped his light. She pushed the theater doors so hard the panels banged into the walls. The loud boom reverberated.

Tom picked up the light and patted the usher's shoulder. "I'm sorry. You're okay?"

When he exited the darkened theater, she was already halfway through the lobby. He caught up with her on the sidewalk. The drizzle had turned into steady rain. She stood on the edge of the curb, getting soaked, one foot in the street, waving for a cab. The heavy traffic was dangerously close.

Tom grabbed her arm and pulled her back. "For God's sake, Rachel."

"Don't. Touch. Me."

It was almost a repeat of the scene with tipsy Billie in the bar, except for the kiss. Rachel was so angry, Tom was sure she would bite him. He held her close and dragged her away from the lights of the marquee, blurry in the downpour, to a patch of relative darkness between two streetlights. The roof overhang provided some shelter. If the scene with Billie could have been mistaken for passion, this one would get him arrested for assault.

"Let me go. I'll scream, I swear."

He pushed her against the wall of the movie theater. "I promised I'd tell you everything. You're going to listen." Her breathing came in short hasty intakes that couldn't supply a lot of air. "Calm down. You'll make yourself dizzy."

"You slept with her."

"I didn't."

She shook her head and tried to squeeze out of his grasp. He didn't give her room to move. She was pinned to the brick wall.

"I wouldn't have to travel all the way to Kansas City to have an affair with Vivian. She has a nice apartment right here in town. I dropped her at it yesterday."

Rachel let out a clucking sound, like the beginning of a hiccup.

"You want the story? You can't use it. I'll deny any of it ever happened."

The expression in her eyes convinced him to release her. She was too curious. She wouldn't run before she got the scoop, publishable or not. He pulled out his cigarettes and lit one. He took a long drag and blew the smoke into the rain.

"Vivian was our undercover agent. I brought her in. I was responsible for her safety."

Rachel stared at him, eyes wide. "Why her?"

"Nobody else could do it. You know how the Mob treats informers."

"How did she gain access?"

Tom leaned on the wall next to her, smoking. Their bodies touched. Rachel didn't move away. "She replaced the girl one of the mobsters hired to accompany him on the trip."

Rachel took a deep breath. "I see."

She was a crime reporter. She knew what kind of role Vivian agreed to play.

"I told you about the contract killer. After the assassination attempt failed, he hid in the hotel spa. Vivian was there, waiting for me, with two other girls. I was going to get them out. The man aimed at Vivian but shot one of the girls instead. When he fired again, he shattered her arm. He was about to finish her off when he was taken down."

"You killed him?"

"I was too late. A kid saved her life, a baby gangster with the proverbial heart of gold."

He took a last puff and crushed the cigarette under his heel. He pondered telling her about Billie and decided that it would only complicate things.

"You could have told me about Vivian when you called, the night you were staring at the ceiling."

"I knew you would be upset. You would have hung up and refused to take my calls, and then you'd run yourself ragged until I came home. And for what? Nothing happened."

"If we hadn't seen this reel, you wouldn't have told me about her."

"That's right. It was a job, a rotten one, and it's over."

Rachel sighed. "I'm sure you're hiding at least half of it, but I won't push my luck." She pulled him off the wall by his suit lapels. She raised on tiptoes and kissed him. "If I'd been behind that newsreel camera, I know who I would have filmed."

"A lousy player who missed all his tries at the ring toss." He smiled. "Ice cream can be awfully distracting." He wrapped an arm around her waist, and she leaned into him.

"We missed the movie," she said.

Tom took off his hat and put it on her head. "You're sopping wet. Bogie can go punch bad guys on his own. I've had my fill of gangsters."

End.

Acknowledgments

Well, we did it again!

We had barely finished writing *Bop City Swing*—the first adventure of Vivian, aka "Gunselle" the professional assassin, and Tom Keegan, the San Francisco PD homicide detective—that we were aching to do it again. When you have characters who play so well together, it is only natural to want them to show what else they can do.

The circumstances are different in *Kansas City Breakdown*. No more chance encounter. Tom and Vivian know each other, know what they are capable of, know their respective strengths and weaknesses.

Not unlike the authors…

The manner in which the story came together was similar this second time around: emails, long conversations, sifting through ideas and themes, secondary characters stepping into the limelight and making such a strong impression that the narrative suddenly curves in new and exciting directions that neither of us foresaw.

We want to thank Adam Van Winkle at Cowboy Jamboree for taking a chance on a follow-up to last year's *Bop City Swing*. It is a pleasure to work with an editor who is also a partner. Warm thanks to Frank Vatel who came up, again, with a killer cover. Sexy, pulpy, just like we like it!

We are infinitely grateful to the writer friends who agreed to read the manuscript in various stages of development. Your comments, insights, and clear-eyed criticism were invaluable. Thank you Carlotta, Michael, Jim for your time and friendship. You gave us food for thought and asked all the right questions. And found a few mistakes on the way … no, you can't call a long-distance number directly from a hotel room in 1952, there's an operator for that!

In closing, we send love to our spouses and partners who are also living, a little bit, on the rebound, with Tom and Vivian. Authors are an obsessive species…

About the Authors

M.E. Proctor was born in Brussels and lives in Texas. She's the author of the Declan Shaw detective mysteries: *Love You Till Tuesday* and *Catch Me on a Blue Day*. She's the author of two short story collections, *Family and Other Ailments* and *A Book to Live By*. She co-wrote two retro-noirs with Russell Thayer: *Bop City Swing* and *Kansas City Breakdown*. Her fiction has appeared in various magazines and anthologies. She's a Shamus Award and Derringer Award short story nominee. You can find more about her at www.shawmystery.com and on https://meproctor.substack.com.

Russell Thayer's work has appeared in *Brushfire, Tough, Roi Fainéant Press, Guilty Crime Magazine, Mystery Tribune, Close to the Bone, Bristol Noir, Apocalypse Confidential, Hawaii Pacific Review, Shotgun Honey, Pistol Jim Press, Rock and a Hard Place Press, Revolution John, Punk Noir, Literary Garage, Expat Press, Pulp Modern, The Yard Crime Blog,* and *Outcast Press. Bop City Swing,* a novel he co-wrote with M.E. Proctor, was published by Cowboy Jamboree Press in 2025. Russell received his BA in English from the University of Washington, worked for decades at large printing companies, and currently lives in Missoula, Montana. You can find him lurking on "X" @RussellThayer10.

www.ingramcontent.com/pod-product-compliance
Lightning Source LLC
LaVergne TN
LVHW090515110826
845146LV00003B/865

* 9 7 9 8 9 0 2 4 3 1 8 3 1 *